BIRD EAT BIRD

BIRD EAT BIRD

Stories by
KATRINA BEST

SEROTONIN | WAYSIDE

INSOMNIAC PRESS

Edited by Jon Paul Fiorentino

Library and Archives Canada Cataloguing in Publication

Best, Katrina, 1966-
    Bird eat bird / Katrina Best.

Short stories.
ISBN 978-1-897178-94-2
    I. Title.
PS8603.E7765B57 2010   C813'.6   C2010-900690-9

The publisher gratefully acknowledges the support of the
Canada Council, the Ontario Arts Council, and the Department
of Canadian Heritage through the Book Publishing Industry De-
velopment Program.

Printed and bound in Canada

Insomniac Press
520 Princess Ave.
London, Ontario, Canada, N6B 2B8
www.insomniacpress.com

   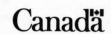

For Alan, Eleanor and Nathaniel

CONTENTS

LUNCH HOUR

The pelican took its time swallowing the pigeon, keeping its mottled prey in the sack of its bill for almost half an hour. At first it held its beak ajar. The gap was wide enough for the smaller bird to escape, but the pigeon just sat there, stupefied, head jerking around occasionally. Perhaps it thought itself lucky to have landed in a cool cave and was admiring the grooved interior whilst enjoying a reprieve from the midday heat on this, the hottest October day on record.

It was the one chance of escape the pigeon would be given. After a couple of minutes, the pelican's bill shut tight. Only then did the doomed bird realize it was somewhere it didn't want to be. A few seconds too late, its survival instincts kicked in. It flapped and fluttered frenetically. Onlookers were horrified.

"Oh Gawd! It's just 'orrible," said one woman. She continued gawking as she took a bite of her chicken and sweetcorn sandwich triangle, part of a Marks & Spencer's variety trio (she had already dispensed with the Wensleydale and carrot, and was saving the prawn cocktail with shredded butter lettuce for afters).

"How on earth did it happen?" said another, popping open a bag of salt and vinegar Discos.

"It just sort of snapped it up, didn't it, Lorraine? Sort of scooped and snapped it up?"

"Yeah. Bloody hell. It's disgusting," said Lorraine.

"But England doesn't have pelicans," said an American tourist. "Does it?"

"Well, it would seem that it does, rather," said a man with a classic Oxbridge accent.

"Yeah, but *wild* ones?" said the American. "I mean, come on! What is this: London, Florida? It must've escaped from the zoo, don't you think?"

"Yes," said a young woman with long hair, bare feet and a beatific smile. "Isn't it great? That poor pelican spent her whole life imprisoned and at last she's found freedom. This is now her home. I think it's wonderful."

"But what about the pigeon?" said a young guy in a vintage suit.

"What pigeon?" said the barefoot young

woman.

"Oh blimey!" cried another office worker. "It's really trying to get out now."

There was a hush as the crowd turned its full attention to the impromptu show. The pelican's bill had begun to quiver and spasm as the pigeon within struck against the walls of its living coffin. The pelican's eyes betrayed no emotion and its bill remained closed.

A man of about forty-five with the weathered skin, red cheeks and crusty, capable hands of a farmer nodded in the direction of the long-haired, barefoot young woman, who was no longer smiling.

"It is wonderful, in't it?" he said, with a northern accent and a wink. "Nature in action. Aye, I'd say it's a privilege to be able t' witness summat like that. A natural wonder."

"Oh really?" The young woman's golden-brown eyes glistened. "First they turf those poor little birds out of Trafalgar Square, and now they're feeding them alive to escaped exotic zoo animals. How exactly is that a natural wonder?" The weather-beaten Yorkshireman didn't respond, other than to wink at her again.

"Anyway," she said to everyone but him, recovering her gentle certainty, "karmic retribution will out. It'll be reborn as a pelican predator."

"Like what?" said an awestruck girl of about twelve in a customized school uniform – she wore her tie on her head like a bandana. "Like, a whale?"

"Maybe a whale," said the young woman indulgently. "Or, maybe, a queen. Or a king, depending on how long its path of destiny takes to unfold."

"What the hell is she going on about?" said Lorraine's friend, finishing her bag of Discos, then blowing it up and popping it with a quick slam of her hands.

"Buggered if I know," said Lorraine.

"Only the Queen is allowed to hunt and eat the swans in her parks," explained the barefoot woman, as if to very small children, or retarded adults.

"Jesus! Is that true?" said Lorraine. "That's disgusting."

"But that's *not* a swan, is it?" said Lorraine's friend.

"No. But our ruling monarch can kill and eat any living thing she finds in one of her parks, any time she wants. It's the law."

"Bloody hell!" said Lorraine. "Any living thing? Because then that would include us, wouldn't it?"

By way of a response, the long-haired woman smiled serenely.

"Fuck me," said Lorraine.

"Whoa, I'm having a total déjà vu," said a boy in his late teens.

"Wicked, mate," said a bicycle courier, who presumably wasn't on a rush delivery.

"I knew you were going to say that," said the teenaged boy.

"I've seen this happen before," said a brisk old lady in a dark trouser suit. A red felt poppy was pinned to her left lapel, even though Remembrance Day was more than three weeks away.

"And that!" said the teenager. "I totally knew she was going to say that."

"Birds were a little different," continued the old lady. "Big one was browner; small one was more of a dove. I'm just trying to work out if it was the summer of fifty-seven or fifty-eight."

"I thought pelicans only liked fish," said a middle-aged woman, her voice rising almost to a wail. "It's so...unnatural. Surely they should only eat fish?"

"Well," said a man with a shaved head and sardonic delivery. "Maybe it's true that pigeons are the fish of the city."

"The other white meat?" suggested another lunchtime comedian.

"Anyone got a match?" said a ruddy city gent who'd staggered into the centre of the park with a pint of real ale and a cigar. "I think I might have swallowed my lighter."

"Still having your déjà vu, mate?" the courier asked the teenaged boy.

"No," he said quietly.

A few people took photos and videos with their mobile phones, but one guy had what looked like a professional camera. The next day it would be revealed that he was a Press Association photographer when one of his shots appeared in every national newspaper in Britain and all over the Internet, alongside a little article describing the unusual spectacle. A staff researcher at the news agency uncovered some obscure facts such as that there are five pelicans currently living on Duck Island in St. James's Park Lake – four Eastern Whites (this was one of those) and one Louisiana Brown – and that they and their ancestors have dwelled there longer than most Londoners, having been introduced as a gift from the Russian Ambassador to King Charles II in 1664. And while a spokesperson for the Royal Society for the Protection of Birds confirmed that pelicans are supposed to eat only fish, it apparently wasn't the first time a St. James's Park pelican had fancied a bit of fowl – one of them had shocked passersby a few years back when it had dined on a duck.

The convulsing bill of the pelican was mesmerizing. By now the large white bird had travelled to the edge of the pond, with its views of Buckingham Palace to the west and the giant wheel of the London Eye to the east. The pelican stood in profile, next to a battered sign which read, "*Do not feed the pelicans.*"

Its pale pink bill was illuminated by the bright sunshine and glittering water causing it to become, almost, translucent, thus accentuating the thrashing silhouette of the trapped pigeon. It was hard not to identify with the writhing dark shadow. The pelican appeared unmoved. It stood calmly on one leg. After a while, it switched to the other leg.

"Oh Christ," said a tearful blonde Australian backpacker.

"What's up, love?" said her boyfriend, trying to put a comforting arm around her, but finding it impossible to reach around her huge purple rucksack.

"Oh, it's just that I can't stop thinking about Steve Irwin, the crazy bastard. I miss him so much."

A tip of the pigeon's wing suddenly emerged, the feathers splayed like dark grey fingers. Some people winced; others leaned forward, stood on tiptoes or held their breath, buoyed by faint hope.

"Oh hurry up and put it out of its misery," said a woman with sunburned shoulders, taking a drag of her Silk Cut cigarette.

"Yes. What the bollocks is it waiting for?" said another.

"Condiments?" said a young man, sniggering at his own joke. Nobody else laughed.

As if it had understood them, the pelican turned and at last faced its audience. Then, as if preparing to laugh raucously, it tipped its head back and tossed its closed bill rapidly and repeatedly until the still-struggling pigeon left its hellish holding sack and was forced head first into the gullet of the larger bird. A few people shuddered and gasped. A little girl screamed and was dragged away by her very pregnant mother. Then all was quiet.

Water trickled from the top of the ornate Victorian fountain. At the lake's edge, in the shade of a weeping willow, which stirred slightly in the humid breeze, two mallards dozed, heads tucked into their plumage.

A woman of about thirty turned to her clutch of colleagues who'd gathered, as was their wont, for a pleasant picnic lunch, happily taking advantage of England's remarkably warm autumn with sandwiches, crisps and iced Frappuccinos in the park.

"Well," she said, slurping the last of her salmon-coloured drink though a fat, white straw. "I suppose that's that, then."

RED

So I'm crossing the street at the busiest downtown intersection and it's so hot I fear my man-
made soles will melt, so I take small, quick steps
across the glistening tarmac, my upper body stiff
as an Irish dancer's. I'm pushing through the
waves of heat and the other side is within reach
when I see a tiny flash of red fall away from the
person in front of me. It bounces once and tum-
bles to rest right in my path. Instinctively, I
move to pick it up – at first I think it's a shiny
jewel – but just before the moment of contact I
recoil. It's a false fingernail, flame red, an oval of
fire on black pitch.

I wonder if I should shout to the owner,
who hasn't yet noticed her loss. She sashays away
on three-inch platinum heels that press into the
spongy road surface, holding for a moment before being sucked up and out again. Her avo-
cado-shaped figure is barely covered by scraps of
clothing: some kind of bustier, a pair of frayed
denim cut-offs. The exposed flesh of her

midriff, smooth as an oil-dipped olive, signals attitude with its brazen, chubby overhang and three tattoos, one of which is giving me the finger. Then she is gone – vanishing into the swaying mirage of heat.

I realize I've been standing here too long and the lights have changed. A driver revs his engine aggressively. I want to kick in his headlights, but I know better than to tangle with road rage and so I move away as the crazy idiot lurches his car forward, just missing me but flattening the false red nail.

It's been one hell of a day so far, and it's not even noon. It started badly and way too early with my lunatic sister Lou – that's short for lunatic – breaking into my apartment. Literally breaking in, I mean, even though she has her own key. She smashed a pane of glass and reached her bare hand in and unlatched my front door claiming she'd lost her key and was worried. About what exactly, she couldn't seem to say. What she did manage to tell me was that she'd tried to call several times, even though we'd spoken less than a day ago. It's not the first time of course, and I doubt it'll be the last. Anyway, if she did try to phone, and it's a big *if*, I wouldn't have heard it ring because I was asleep and had my earplugs in. I have to wear them because the noise downtown is worse than ever these days, and in the summer I have to keep the windows open or I'd get heatstroke. And she knows that. Anyway, she said she'd jumped to all sorts of bad conclusions and had come racing over and started knocking on the door and ringing the bell, which I also didn't hear on account of the earplugs if, and it's another big *if*, she actually did ring the bell and knock on the door before breaking in. The crazy bitch, she's been losing it more often lately – I suspect she might need to get her meds readjusted. Poor thing's had it rough, though, what with that husband of hers just up and leaving like that, not that you can blame him.

Anyway, she's lucky she didn't slit her wrist breaking that glass, unless maybe that was the idea. She's always been a total fuck-up. I told her she was paying to replace the glass, and she couldn't argue with that. And then I promised I'd get her another key cut. Even though she'll probably just lose it again. The key and her mind. You've got to laugh, really, or you'll cry, that's what Mom always said. And it's true.

So that's what I'm doing now – getting yet another key cut for my sister. I left her at the apartment to wait for the window repair guys to come, even though I wasn't thrilled about leaving her there alone. I thought it would only take ten minutes to get the key cut, fifteen tops, as there's a little store at the end of my street with an old guy who cuts keys and mends shoes. He also sells cheap bags. But when I got there this morning the store was boarded up. So now I have to try and find another place, and as quickly as possible so I can get back home before Lou pulls another of her crazy stunts.

I lunch at an underground food court, enjoying the air conditioning but not the heat-lamped falafel plate. I reach the end of my Orange Crush and a shard of ice shoots up through the straw and into my throat where it wedges tight. I am choking silently, winded and wincing and thinking the ice should surely melt. Or is my throat not warm enough? Could a person die this way in the middle of the day in the middle of a busy mall devoid of natural light? I haven't made a will, but then again, I only have debts to bequeath and my sister is welcome to them. And there's Tommy, my cat; I should think of a more reliable guardian for him. What bothers me most is the thought of Lou going through my stuff. As I'm cursing my lifelong tendency to hoard and procrastinate, the ice chip dislodges and I cough it up and crunch it into liquidity and breathe again and notice an old lady watching me. I give her a reassuring wave.

"I'm okay," I call to her. I realize I need to use the bathroom.

A fold-out yellow sign announces that the women's washrooms are being cleaned. I read the warning as I glide across a patch of wet floor and bang! straight into the disabled stall, thus bypassing the queue of jittery women. This seems fortuitous until I notice there is someone already seated on the extra high toilet. I'm processing this information as I land in her wheelchair, face first. I don't know what to say.

"Hello," I say. "*Ça va?*"

"I'm in here," she replies, redundantly.

"I slipped on the wet floor," I say. "The door wasn't locked." I try not to sound too accusatory, as it's not yet been established that the lock is operational. I notice her withered legs hanging, useless. I look at mine, not exactly those of a supermodel but certainly functional and, being empathetic, I suddenly have the urge to commiserate about the lack of disabled accessibility in the city.

"Montreal sucks for access, doesn't it?" I say. "I've noticed that there are several intersections where there's no lowering of the curb whatsoever. It's outrageous!" She doesn't respond, I figure because she agrees. She's probably shy, too. I used to be shy, but I learned how to make good small talk and put people at ease. It's something people have often complimented me on over the years. Some people let uncomfortable silences ruin everyone's day; sometimes I've even met people who cause them on purpose. I'm the opposite of that. She's staring at me, as if waiting for me to say something else of interest.

"In Vancouver, it's way better," I tell her. "They have ramps everywhere and bird whistles for deaf people at all the crosswalks. The whistling lasts as long as the *Walk* sign, then when it stops flashing, the chirruping stops too. The different bird sounds tell you where you are in the city – every crosswalk has its own unique chirp. It's quite the innovation, isn't it?"

"Bird whistles for deaf people?" she says, and I can detect a little sarcasm in her voice, which is known to be the lowest form of wit. But in her case, it's more likely a form of defence, poor thing.

"Oh right, you're right. What is it now?

Hearing impaired?"

"Bird whistles for people who can't *hear*? I think you must mean for the blind."

"Oh, good catch! Except I think we're meant to say 'seeing impaired'? Or 'sight challenged.' Anyway, it's awesome out there."

Her silence makes me feel a little uncomfortable, but I'm determined not to get resentful. We all have our crosses to bear.

"Seriously, there are ramps everywhere in Vancouver. Really, it's fantastic."

Finally, she opens her mouth to say something.

"So why don't you go the fuck back to Vancouver then?" she says.

I'm about to explain why I don't want to go the fuck back to Vancouver, but something in her eyes tells me she doesn't really care to know. I'm quite instinctual like that. So I decide to overlook her social ineptitude and simply leave. As I stumble out, I test the lock, which is too stiff for me to slide. (I have very strong fingers. Only once have I encountered a jar that I couldn't open. Even wearing my thickest pair of rubber gloves it wouldn't budge. Baby dill pickles. I ended up having to smash it open on the hearth, then used a piece of the broken glass to spear them, which saved washing a fork.)

I try again but the lock won't budge. So there *is* something wrong with it. I smile at her one last time, but she doesn't reciprocate. Some people are just like that. It's too bad for them – smile at the world and it smiles back at you, I once heard. It's a little bit true. But it's also true that some people are so committed to being miserable that they wouldn't smile if a life-sized Raggedy Ann doll leaped up and asked them to dance.

I try to pull the door closed, but it swings open again. I think about holding it closed for her until she's ready to come out, but I really need to pee. So I leave the door as it is, and join the end of the line.

At last it's my turn. Once inside the toilet stall, I carefully remove my prescription sunglasses from my head and put them on the flat top of the paper dispenser. Too many times I haven't done this and have had them either fall down over my eyes, cutting off my vision, or worse, fall right down onto my undies, which then act like a trampoline, bouncing them off onto the filthy floor, or worse, onto the filthy floor of the stall next door. Along with my social skills, one of my best characteristics is how well and quickly I learn from my mistakes.

As I exit the stall I'm almost knocked over by two children who appear as desperate to use the toilet as I was. It's a brother and sister, the boy an overfed five or six, the girl maybe nine – skinny legs, rounded belly and barrel chest in a glittery miniskirt, tight baby T and cropped denim jacket with the word *Angel* on the back in pink stitching accented with diamanté.

"Hey, slow down, kiddies," I say. I'm admonishing them, but they know it's not serious because I also chuckle affectionately. I'm good with children, older ones anyway – babies do tend to cry when I pet them. But that's mostly because they're not yet accustomed to having their souls scrutinized.

As soon as I hear the bolt click shut I remember my sunglasses, which I left on top of the toilet roll dispenser. It feels like they're still on top of my head, but when I put my hand up to check, there's only hair. Still, I look in the mirror in case I might catch sight of the phantom shades. No such luck, but I do notice my grey roots are back. It's as if someone painted a fat stripe down my parting, but that's not literally what happened. I'm reminded of a skunk or that bad lady in that cartoon film with all the spotted dogs. I remember liking that movie and I like skunks quite a lot, but I don't particularly want to look like one. If I had to pick an animal to be, I'd choose a giraffe. I check my pockets just in case I put the sunglasses away without realizing it, but it's no surprise to find they're empty.

The mother of the two children wears faded leggings and a horizontally striped top that exposes her needle-sharp shoulders. She leans against the door to their stall, conversing with her offspring as they take turns using the toilet. I watch her reflected in the mirror as I wash and rinse my hands three times. I continue to watch her as I dry my hands under the hygienic "no touch" dryer, which doesn't come alive until I've given it four bashes with my wet fist.

The children are in the stall a long time. The mother stops conversing with them and starts yelling.

"Right! Two more minutes. Jacob, did you lift the seat?"

"Yeah, Mom."

"Gabrielle-Ange, lift the seat for your brother!"

"I did! We're almost done."

"One minute! Or I'll start counting, I swear.

You hear me? *Un...deux...*"

"*Oui, Maman.* Almost finished."

Finally the toilet flushes, the door opens and out they spill, giggling and fake-wrestling with each other. I barge back in before the next in line can (luckily it's a really old chick, all wizened and bent over and super slow) and reach for my sunglasses but they're no longer on the dispenser. I look on the floor, under each of the two neighbouring stalls and, finally, in the toilet itself. Nothing. Feeling a bit like I'm in a movie scene, I burst back out just as the little kleptomaniacs and their crackhead of a mother are leaving the washroom.

"Excuse me! Excuse me, Madam!" She turns, rough faced and uncaring. Her little monsters chase each other nearby.

"Yes?"

"Your children have taken my sunglasses."

"What?"

"In the washroom. The toilet stall. I left my sunglasses on the toilet paper holder."

"So?"

"Just before they went in. I was in there right before them. And I went back in right after they came out. I looked everywhere... They're the only ones who could have taken"

"Are you accusing my kids of stealing?"

"Yes. It's the only explanation. Unless there's a magician in here."

"Well, that's probably it, then, isn't it?"

"No, it's much more likely that your kids took them."

"Or maybe *you're* the magician and you magicked them into wherever bunnies and shit wind up when they vanish."

"No, I'm not a magician," I say, which is sort of true.

"Lady, go fuck yourself. Jacob, Gabrielle-Ange, *allons-y!*" And with that, she bustles them out. I watch them go, incredulous. I don't get shocked that easily, but that potty-mouthed mother shocked the hell out of me! I consider putting a curse on her, but I don't know how, even though I'm often told I look very much like I'm capable of that kind of thing and I secretly think maybe I am. I own a deck of tarot cards, which I like to shuffle sometimes and deal out and look at as a way of relaxing. They're very pretty.

On the bus home I almost sit on a little person, who turns out to be mildly schizophrenic – he says he's just come back from the doctor's and finally got a proper diagnosis and wants to talk about it. His name is Wayne. I'm compelled to listen; it's the least I can do, besides he has a dreamy English accent and is very articulate. I used to be a total Anglophile, but got over it when I spent an afternoon with a bricklayer from Portsmouth who was so boring I fell asleep.

Wayne says he's from "Norf-East London" – a place called Barking. And he's not boring. He's very sweet, although he's also quite bitter about a lot of things, mostly the fact that his little girlfriend just ran off with his best little friend. He's understandably fallen off the wagon and wants company. He suggests I come for a drink with him at his local pub.

"It's a nice boozer, *The Rose and Crown*," he says. "Almost like the real thing back home except you have lager, pool and pretzels instead of beer, billiards and crisps. Actually they do have one real ale on tap, but bugger me if the beer doesn't come out ice cold and with practically no head, so that's no effing good. You'd think I'd get used to it, but some things stick with you.

But that's okay; I can enjoy a nice pint of lager too, 'specially in the heat. Goes better with pork scratchings in a way, not that you can get 'em here. Lunch isn't quite right either, but they do their best. No ploughman's, more's the pity. Plenty of tasty tarts, though, 'specially on a Tuesday for some reason, and a dart board too, and a fair few dust-ups to keep things interesting, so it's quite a lot like the real thing, innit?"

I don't really have a clue what he's talking about but have often passed by *The Rose and Crown* pub and wondered what it's like inside. I'm happy to listen to Wayne for the entire sixteen stops of my bus journey but decline the offer of a drink. I don't want to lead him on, poor little fellow. I look out the window as he chats away, knowing he's telling his clever anecdotes to my cleavage. That's one thing about me that's classically incredible. I'm glad I wore my push-up bra and a low-cut top today – one of my own designs, made from a plain grey T-shirt. I've always been quite creative and very handy with a pair of scissors. My mother used to call me "Crafty Christina," which probably seems a little strange seeing as my name is really Maureen. But it's quite common amongst witching families to have a real given name and a secret name, to make it harder for our enemies to put curses on the children.

Suddenly I see the potty-mouthed mother and her brats walking along the road.

"Hey!" I yell, banging on the window.

"What is it? What's happened?" Wayne asks.

"Someone I have unfinished business with," I explain. "I have to go. Stop the bus!"

I rise and nearly fall again as the bus rounds a corner too fast. The driver is one of those officious types and refuses to stop his bus until the next actual stop. He pretends not to even notice me, but I see his miserable face in the rear-view and show it my stiff middle finger as I leap off and half-run in the direction of that terrible mother and her two venomous children.

"Hey! Hey, Lady! *Madame!* Hey! Wait up! *Attention!*"

She turns around and our eyes lock, or they would except she's now wearing high-end designer sunglasses with polarized lenses and a prescription for astigmatism in the left eye, so I can't actually see hers. I see her legs, though, starting to move, faster, faster, and her arms, hurrying her children along, urging them to bolt. Her hands get busy too – each one grabs a brat and starts hauling it along. I give chase, but after a few blocks of trying to sprint in my turquoise espadrille wedges, I realize it's hopeless. I stop and instead say a small, quiet incantation. After that I feel much better and smile to myself. Perhaps I do, after all, possess the gift. She and her thieving juvies are going to regret stealing my sunglasses, I can feel it.

I should go home but figure the day can't get any worse, and perhaps it can get a little better in *The Rose and Crown* authentic British pub. I wouldn't know if it's close to the real thing or not, as I've never been to the United Kingdom. I've never been abroad, in fact, unless you count the Island of Prince Edward, and frankly, I no longer do.

Wayne is very happy to see me and offers me some of his Guinness, which he says he ordered because he forgot to eat lunch. He asks for cutlery and spoons it into his mouth like soup. I order a pint of blanche, which comes with a slice of lemon. I offer the fruit to Wayne as a refreshing dessert. He sucks on it gratefully, winking at me a little.

He turns out to be quite the character, really witty, especially after a couple of drinks. And knowledgeable. Wow. He says he always wins at

Trivial Pursuit and was supposed to be on the British version of *Who Wants to Be a Millionaire?* He apparently got through all the rounds on the phone, but the producers got scared about putting a little person on. They gave him some line about how cushions weren't allowed due to their being a fire hazard.

"I thought they was pulling me plonker at first," he says. "Then when I realized they wasn't jesting, I was going to sue 'em, but then I couldn't be arsed. Talk about pants."

"I'm sorry," I say. I'm reacting to his sad expression. I still don't understand most of what he says.

"*Pop Idol*'s the same," he says. "I'm too old now, 'course, but even if I'd auditioned when I was young enough, I would've got nowhere fast. It don't matter which country you watch it in, the finalists are always full-sized. Sometimes they're more than flipping full-sized; sometimes they're double-sized. But they are never, ever half-sized."

I'd never thought about it before, but the little smartie is right. After that, Wayne just gets more and more fascinating. He wonders why sandwich shop workers bother putting on plastic gloves to make the sandwiches since they then keep them on when they're handling the money.

"Which everyone knows is filthy, hence, the expression 'filthy lucre,'" he says. "Where's the frigging hygiene?" he asks, and I have to tell him I have no idea.

My bar stool doesn't have padding and I've lost all the feeling in my buttocks, so I suggest we move from the bar to a table by the wall, which is exposed brick. Looking at him set against that wall, it's like having my own little stand-up comedian, except he's sitting, and of course even if he were standing he'd appear to be sitting, at least from a distance. He wonders why brides always grow their hair for their weddings.

"They spend months growing it out, then on the big day, poof! They bleeding put it up!"

"Do they?"

"Yeah, so what's the effing point? It makes their ears stick out and then they get the photos back and start crying. And then the jammy sods try and blame the effing photographer." Turns out Wayne used to be a wedding photographer's assistant, and part of his job was to get the bride and groom to sign a release form acknowledging their physical flaws.

He's so observant I'm in awe, that's when

I'm not in stitches. He's hilarious, but also insightful. He wonders why people have trouble remembering to say "little people" instead of "midget" or "dwarf." He explains that there are big differences between these categories that no regular-sized person can fully appreciate.

"There are two hundred categories of dwarfism," he explains. "And mine is the two hundred and first." He bemoans the demise of the freak show because, he says, guys like him could earn a decent living in show business back then. He sometimes works as an extra on movies and says a couple of years ago he took part in a private dwarf-tossing event held by a billionaire on a private island in a lake in the countryside. Apparently, Wayne was handled by too many celebrities to list. But only one dropped him. A female, first name Celine, is all he'll tell me. I need a bit more to go on, but he just smiles and says, "Mum's the word."

"Go on," I say. "Was she gorgeous?"

"Face like a bag of spanners," he replies. "Good body though. And you wouldn't have guessed she'd have fingers like pig's tits. It hurt like hell at the time, but what are you going to do? She was very sorry. Made up for it with a nice cash bonus. The bruises went away after a couple of weeks, so I wasn't complaining."

He says business hasn't been great since the markets crashed but he still has his connections and plans to look some of them up and offer his services at celebrity parties.

"I'm like that Hollywood madam with the A-list contacts," he tells me. "Have to store me little black book in a safety deposit box. It's got numbers people would kill for, including Tom's mobile." At first I assume it's that nutbar Tom Cruise, but then I remember Tom Hanks. And, of course, Tom Thumb.

"It's quite small but I keep it clean," Wayne is saying. I'm pretty sure he's talking about his apartment, and I decline his invitation due to a prior commitment.

"Sorry," I say. "I can't go home with you. I already have a date tonight." He manages to hide his disappointment quite well, but then again, he's probably used to rejection, poor little chap. I ask him to write his number down and promise to call him if my date doesn't work out. He seems grateful for that ray of hope at least. I'm not lying. I do have a date in a couple of hours, a blind date, though not literally "sight impaired," as far as I know.

I get home and the door is ajar. There's nobody around but the cat. There's still some food in his bowl, like some miracle worker has been around. Then I remember what happened this morning. The glass seems to have been fixed and Lou's left a note, which isn't even legible. She's left a bottle of pills next to the note. I shake it – almost full, phew. So the crazy bitch hasn't tried to off herself that way. Not this time, anyway. I suddenly remember her yelling this morning, yelling about the pills as I was leaving. Shaking the bottle after me, *shake shake shake*. I suddenly remember the key – I forgot to get one cut. Well, I didn't exactly forget. I just didn't come across a place yet. Maybe I'll find one tonight, that's open late.

I go to the bathroom and, looking in the mirror, wonder if I have time to do something about my hair. I think about wearing a hat, but they make me sweat. I don't have any regular hair dye, but I do have an old tub of shoe polish that's pretty close to my natural shade. It goes on surprisingly well – I'm careful not to spread it too thick – and it adds shine (which I guess is only to be expected) as well as colour. I'm very pleased with the results.

Next I choose my outfit. I'm wearing my

best pants already, they're checkered blue and brown and pink and no longer have creases down the middle but still look pretty sharp. I remember how well my top worked on Wayne earlier, and so I keep that on too. I decide to accessorize and choose a pretty yellow ribbon that I found tied to a sapling in the park. It looks cute against my shiny black-brown hair, tied in a bow. There's enough extra length to tie around my neck too. I look pretty and summery, what with the turquoise espadrilles and all. I hope it doesn't rain.

I only own one item of makeup, a rich red lipstick. A real professional makeup artist called Mary Kay once told me that one item is all you need if you know how to use it. I apply the lipstick first to my cheeks as rouge, enhancing my natural bone structure, then dab and spread a little below my eyebrows and put a lot on my lips. I blot them on the back of my hand, and seeing the imprint of my own lips turns me on a little. I look at my reflection and giggle. I like what I see.

On the way to the park I find a dollar. The day appears to be looking up. I stop at the dep on the corner and spend my lucky loonie on a scratch-and-win instant lottery ticket. I no longer have a coin, obviously, because I used it to pay for the ticket, so instead I use my nails to scratch away all the silver squares. I can't believe it when I see three little critters, which, according to the legend at the bottom of the ticket, means I've won two dollars. I check three times to make sure, then hand it to the young clerk.

"I've won two bucks," I tell him. Some of these kids can't even read these days.

"Yeah, but it's void," he says. "You've scratched all the squares, not just three. And you've scratched the area is says not to scratch or else it's void. Look."

"Well, of course I scratched all of the squares," I say. "Come on! Who doesn't?" Of course it's impossible, once you've started scratching, to resist removing every bit of the silver. Then you have to blow the bits away until they cease to exist. I begin to wonder if the young man is just a bit slow, or totally cuckoo. I decide to tread carefully.

"I won and I want my two dollars, please," I say slowly and politely. He doesn't answer but reaches below the counter, and next thing I know two enormous Chinese men are carrying me out of the store. They dump me on the sidewalk and tell me never to come back, as if I'd want to. When did the Asians get so tall? I should've known a day like today wouldn't really get any better.

When I get to the park, Maggie from downstairs is already there, feeding the pigeons. It looks like she's giving them frozen waffles, the dozy dame.

"Those look like frozen waffles, Maggie!" I call to her. "What the hell are you doing?"

"They love the Eggos," she calls back.

"I love the Eggos too!" yells one of the guys from the halfway house across the street. I look him up and down. He's a bit hairy, but not in bad shape. I wonder if that's who I'm meeting. Going by the day I've had so far, I doubt it. Someone's left a bagel on the bench. It's still soft enough to pull apart, so I join Maggie in feeding the birds. A black squirrel with half a tail comes out of the garbage and begs for a piece. I throw a lump its way and it picks it up in its cute little front paws and daintily nibbles the sesame seeds. I've always loved nature, it makes me feel at peace somehow and animals are easy to talk to. I don't even mind the rats and cockroaches, although they rarely stick around for an entire conversation.

My date never shows. Still, I sit there until it's really dark. A few of the guys are passing a bottle around and mouthing off over by the statue. Normally I'd join in, but I'm feeling a little pissed off about my date's lack of respect, although of course it's possible he didn't make it due to illness or death or something. It's also possible I got the day wrong. Funny thing is, as I'm sitting there, I realize I don't care. I can't stop thinking about Wayne. I pull his number out and head for the phone booth. I dial the operator and tell her my quarters got stuck then give her Wayne's number to try. She tells me it doesn't work.

"That's impossible," I say. "Try again." She tries three more times.

"It's not in service," she says again. "I'm sorry, Madam." The line goes dead. I finally twig that she was deliberately dialling it wrong because she didn't totally believe me about the quarters. She may even have been watching me on a hidden camera. As I hang up the phone, I flip her the bird and stick my tongue out. Then I blow a raspberry just in case there's a hidden mic in there too. I decide to see if Wayne's still at the pub.

The Rose and Crown is noisier and busier than it was earlier. I finally spot Wayne over at the far side of the bar, just visible beside a fruit machine. I wave at him and he disappears. As I suspected, the poor little guy is legless. Not literally, of course, that's just a figure of speech. No, he still has legs, albeit short ones, but they're not serving him too well tonight. I go over and haul him up and press his head into my cleavage. I hold him there tight. The hug feels great. He's making muffled sounds, but I can't make out the words, so I pull him out again. He looks up at me, blinking.

"Yes, Wayne, it's really me, Mo," I say. "I came back for you, honey."

"Blimey! What the bleeding hell did you do to your face?" he says.

"Trade secret," I say with a wink. I love flirting. I crouch down so I'm at his level.

"Flipping Nora!" he exclaims. "What's that on your head?"

"Like it?" I say, winking. He leans in and smells it, reacts dramatically.

"What is it?" he says, wrinkling his nose in really the cutest way.

"A girl can't give away her beauty secrets," I say. I'm being coy and he's loving it.

"Fuck me," says Wayne. "I need another drink."

"Me too," I say. "Your place or mine?"

"What?" he says. "Oh! No offence, darling, but I usually only get off with little people. Or redheads, in a pinch. Thanks for the offer, though. Appreciate it." I feel very flattered that he called me darling. He looks again at my newly darkened hair, can't seem to take his eyes off it, so I move my head gently from side to side, knowing the lights will give it extra sheen, hoping that it sparkles and hypnotizes him a little.

"I thought you were a bit puddled earlier," he says. "But now I can see you are completely puggled."

"Thank you," I say, flashing him my sexiest smile.

Of course I do understand about needing to

stick with your own kind. Plus, the way Wayne talks, he's such a learned little gentleman. He's not really being a bigot – he has his pride and we both know I'm out of his league. Or, at least, out of his comfort zone – too much woman for him to handle.

I find an empty glass and fill it from an abandoned pitcher of *rousse*. I stay for quite a while, but at last call, I decide to get out. There's a chill in the air, and although the sky is still dark, I can sense the damp approach of morning. Perhaps I'll get out my tarot cards when I get home; I do find them so comforting. I'm good at shuffling and dealing, and one of these days I hope to use them to make some money, if only I can first get over my aversion to the Cups family.

I reach a major intersection and stop. I look up towards the dark shadow of Mount Royal and see the lit-up cross. For the first time in years I think about praying, but I've forgotten how to, like I've forgotten how to cry. My scalp suddenly starts itching and burning like it's been set alight. I suddenly have a vague recollection about being allergic to shoe polish. I reach up to scratch the irritated area and my fingers close on something at the back of my head. It's my sunglasses, apparitions no more! I can hardly believe it. I put them on just to make sure they're real.

Even though it's nighttime, my vision improves at once. The cross up on the mountain is glowing now and the lights aren't just white, but multicoloured, like fairy lights. In the distance is the musical wail of a siren. Suddenly there's the screeching of brakes and a car pulls up. A woman gets out. She looks a bit like my mother and she's yelling my name. I start to run, but she grabs me and tries to force something down my throat, then pours water into my mouth. Crazy bitch! I spit it out along with the soggy pink tablet.

"What the fuck?" I cry.

"You need to take these, Maureen," she says. "You're hours overdue now. Where have you been? Everyone's been worried sick."

Then I realize. It's just like when I was little and got the shoe polish on my arm and welts came up and Mom raced me to the doctor and then took care of it. She's giving me the shoe polish antidote.

"Is it the shoe polish antidote?" I say.

"Do you want it to be?" she replies, which makes absolutely no sense.

"What the fuck does that mean? Of course I want it to be. My head feels like it's on fucking fire."

"Then yes," she says, holding out two of the pink pills and a bottle of water. "It's the shoe polish antidote. Here, take two."

I take the two pills from her, toss them into my mouth and chase them down with the water.

"Did you get the key cut?" she says.

"Not yet. How did you know about that anyway?"

"Let me drive you home," she says. "It's really late."

"That's not a great idea, Mom," I say. "You have night blindness, remember?"

"It's Lou," says Mom, but she's mistaken. There's only the two of us here. Poor Mom, I think she might be beginning to lose her marbles as well as her eyesight.

Suddenly I notice the round green light across the deserted intersection. And there, beneath it, is the little white man, shining, luminescent. I think of Wayne and smile. I wait for a second, expecting him to start singing like an angel or telling jokes, but he doesn't. Instead he transforms into an orange hand, which beckons to me, flashing rhythmically. I step out. Halfway across I see something on the road – no, not really on, it's *in* the road. And I realize that I am ✻ back where the day began. For there, embedded in asphalt, is the glossy red ellipse, that devil's teardrop, winking at the dawn.

AT SEA

The Cope-Gagnon family wound its way along the beach. It was just after ten in the morning and already the white sand was almost hot. Carol paused to put on her sandals and help her two children into their beach shoes, while her husband, Martin, remained barefoot and strode heroically ahead. Carol brushed the sand from her toddler's soles before guiding his soft little feet into emerald green moulded plastic sandals.

The mile-long stretch of sand was filling up fast. Dozens of other families had already staked out their spots for the day with brightly coloured parasols, blankets and towels. In the distance, Carol could just make out the barbed wire fence that divided this renowned Coronado Cays bathing beach from a deserted, but otherwise identical, stretch of waterfront that belonged to the US Navy.

"Here, Mummy, this looks good," said Abby.

"It's a bit close to the waterline, darling," said Carol, but she stopped, dropped her overstuffed tote bag and let go of two-year-old Charlie's hand. Martin walked back to join them and dumped their cooler and beach umbrella on the sand, then swung the large knapsack from his shoulders.

"I think the tide is still coming in," said Martin.

"What's tide, Mummy?" said Abby.

"Ask Daddy. He's better than me at explaining scientific things."

"Daddy, what's tide?"

"The nation's favourite detergent," said Daddy, prompting Mummy to hit him in the gut with the rolled up beach mat.

Carol noticed how much Martin's stomach protruded now and how it wobbled when hit. She also noticed how young women still seemed to find him – and his love handles – attractive. Even when he was showcasing his flab in his baggy old beach trunks with his harried wife and two small children in tow, she could sense his admirers watching him – their oversized sunglasses flashed as he walked by.

"This is a perfect example of what we discussed last night, Martin."

"In what way? Last night you were freaking out over the gingerbread man scene. I mean, for fu—dgicle's sake." She knew it was her stern look that had made him change course mid-sentence. She wished wielding that kind of influence made her feel good. She tried to remember what their marriage guidance counsellor had said, about not engaging in power struggles, about doing the opposite and meeting him halfway and remembering to show her appreciation for the little things, even if she didn't *feel* all that appreciative at the time, even if the reasons she *didn't* feel appreciative were totally valid.

"Thank you, Martin," she said.

"What for?"

"For managing to self-monitor so effectively."

"Self-monitor so effectively? We've been in California two minutes and already you're spouting psychobabble."

"Oh fudge off." They glared at each other. Carol had already forgotten what had provoked this argument.

"Look," said Martin, bringing it back to topic and showing that *he* had not forgotten, he with the superior memory, "you are never going to convince me that a computer-generated cartoon of a gingerbread man—" Ah yes, now she remembered.

"A gingerbread man being *tortured*, Martin."

"By another *cartoon*... Never mind, forget it. Let's just agree to disagr—"

"No, actually, let's not. I know that on some level you know I'm right. No child should see a film like *Shrek* before she knows the classics which it is parodying. And anyway, five is too young to have to deal with irony, let alone sarcasm."

"Who's being sarcastic?"

"Just answer her properly, please. She's a sponge right now; she wants to learn. Is it too much to ask that we please just respect and honour that?"

"Why don't *you* answer her, Carol? I can't be trusted to stick to the approved script. I might be tempted to say something contentious. Or funny. God forbid."

"Please don't use the 'G' word. We might not be religious, but we are holidaying in the United States. We don't want to become targets." A faint rumbling made them look up and, as if choreographed, a sinister looking, unmarked black aircraft flew low overhead. It was an odd shape, darkly futuristic – part hexagon, part stingray.

"Airplane!" cried Abby excitedly, adding uncertainly, "Is it?"

Carol and Martin exchanged a look that threatened to unite them. Carol felt herself softening and fought the urge to smile. Instead she turned on her husband with an exaggerated frown.

"That was a fudging warplane, Martin. I knew we should've rented that cabin in BC."

"Oh yes, that's just great. You've been lobbying to go to San Diego since last Christmas, but now we're finally here, go ahead and blame me for forcing you into it."

"You're unbelievable, you know that?"

"You're wasting precious time and energy, dearest," said Martin. "Our daughter is still waiting for a serious explanation about what the tide is, remember, so I suggest you give her one."

Carol turned to Abby who had long since stopped listening to her parents and was attempting to crush a baby crab with the sharp corner of her shovel.

"Don't hurt the sea creatures, sweetie," said Carol, gently prizing the shovel from her daughter's fist, then squatting down in order to look right into her eyes, which were cornflower blue with flecks of amber around the edges, just like Martin's.

"Now then, Abby," she said in a loud, clear

voice. "I am going to answer your wonderful question about what the tide is, okay? Let me see now. Okay, so the sea – the ocean – has tides. They come in and go out. So the water comes in and goes out too, and it's somehow linked to the waxing and waning of the moon, but that's not really—"

"Look!" yelled Abby. "A starfish! Is it dead?"

"Don't touch it, honey... Where's Charlie? Oh Jesus! Martin! Where's Charlie?"

"Right over there. Take a chill pill, would you?"

"Oh dear God, he's eating cigarette butts again. Quick, Martin, go get him. Quick!"

"Relax, he's fine. So he likes eating crap. It'll build up his immunity."

"Right, yes, that's just fantastic. He's ingesting nicotine and cyanide and fudge knows what else. That's really going to stave off—"

"You know, Carol, when you use the word *fudge* in that way, it stops sounding innocuous."

Turning her body so her back was to her children, Carol gave her husband the finger.

"All right, all right, I'll go get him," said Martin and he set off across the warm white sand to retrieve their wandering toddler.

"Ow!" cried Abby. "It bit me."

"Don't be silly, darling," said Carol. "Starfish don't bite, especially if they're dead."

"That one did. I need a Princess bandage."

"All right, sweetie, sit here." Carol scooped Abby up and plopped her on the cooler box. Abby grizzled and wriggled her toes into the sand. Carol zipped open the first aid kit. "Okay, I'll find you a bandage, but I think there's only SpongeBob left."

"Nooooo!" wailed Abby. "I want a Princess."

"SpongeBob or plain. That's all I have, Abby, I'm sorry."

Abby stuck her lip out in a sulky pout. "Princess!"

"Right, then I guess the boo-boo isn't that bad," said Carol, slowly and deliberately putting away the home-assembled first aid kit, which was lacking nail scissors – the pair she'd used for the past ten years had been confiscated (gleefully, she couldn't help noticing) by the airport security official, along with a bottle of dye free, grape flavoured, liquid acetaminophen and an oversized tube of whitening toothpaste.

Looking her daughter in the eye, Carol zipped the bag shut.

"Okay then, SpongeBob," said Abby, as if she were doing her mother a favour.

As she peeled away the sticky bandage's backing, Carol wondered how the fuck she had got here. She used to be the one saying clever, sarcastic things all day long, encouraging Martin to engage in verbal sparring with her. It was a form of foreplay for them both. His affectionate teasing had attracted her instantly, and she'd especially loved that he wasn't afraid to show his dark side, and didn't seem to be afraid when she showed hers. He had an edge. She had an edge. They were all about the edge when they were first married. They both lived on it, for fuck's sake, spending their last five bucks on tax-free smokes bought from vendors on the beach. They dressed in edgy clothes, said edgy things and hung out with an edgy crowd of counter-culture people who dressed primarily in black. For a couple of years they had shared meals, joints and entire weekends with those people but, she now realized, had kept in touch with none of them.

These days, the last thing she wanted was edge. She wanted consistency and calm and companionship, a family-centered life, though obviously with some excitement too, just not the kind born of anxiety. She no longer marched for causes, but she did sign plenty of online petitions and forwarded pre-written emails to Members of Parliament. Because of course she still wanted world peace and global social programs and true democracy and the reversal of global warming and the eradication of the extreme disparity between rich and poor, although admittedly she also wanted to be able to afford a new kitchen and private school for the kids – not that she'd actually *send* them to one, but having the choice would be nice. Lately she'd been having a recurring fantasy about becoming a "Mompreneur" and producing a new must-have item for babies and toddlers that would net her a fortune, if only she knew how to sew.

She wanted a real partner who supported her in everything, someone who was firmly on her side no matter what. She suspected that Martin did too, and if they weren't so tired and worn down they might mutually realize the irony of this and laugh and make everything all right again. She did miss laughing, and she missed being funny, but being funny and being a good mother didn't seem to go together, although her own mother had managed to bring up three children in a tiny bungalow in Crawley without sacrificing her offbeat sense of humour.

"This will seem sentimental and clichéd when you're older. Never mind, I do appreciate the effort," her mum had said when Carol, aged seven, had presented her with a handmade Mother's Day card – a misshapen heart, some flowers, a seven-band Crayola rainbow and three lines of hugs and kisses. She'd written inside, "*To Mummy, the best mother in the hole world. I love you. Love from Carol.*" Her mother, who was breastfeeding Carol's new baby brother at the time, had tossed it aside with an exaggerated eye roll, but also a smile, which Carol had found confusing. Carol's eleven-year-old sister Laura, who'd been watching smugly from the doorway, had then brought over her offering: a blank card with a short note on the outside, printed in simple black letters, which read, "*This card has been redacted to protest the over-commercialization of Mother's Day.*" Their mother had thrown back her head and laughed. Then she had grabbed her elder daughter and squeezed her awkwardly for a couple of seconds.

"That's my girl," Mum had said.

"Sad!" said Charlie, taking a fistful of sand and shoving it in his mouth. "Sad sad Mama." She'd weaned him just a couple of weeks before this trip. She hadn't really meant to – in fact, since he was almost certainly going to be their last baby, she'd thought she might let him breastfeed until he started kindergarten. But he'd turned away from her nipple one night, and again the following morning, and that had been that.

"Right, let's move then," said Martin.

"What? Why? We just got settled."

"Didn't you hear the announcement? There's a riptide here, we need to move along the shoreline a bit, closer to the next lifeguard tower."

"Nonsense. The waves look pretty gentle. People are still having fun right here." She pointed in front of them – at least a dozen people were in the water, wading, swimming and boogie boarding.

"But look over there, where it's brown under the white caps. See? That's the riptide," Martin said.

"Like an undertow you mean?"

"Actually, no, that's different. People often mix them up. "

"Oh really? And how come you're such an

expert?"

"I worked as a lifeguard when I was younger." Carol looked at her husband with genuine surprise. How could she not have known this? After thirteen years together, they knew all each other's stories.

"Did you? Where?"

"Ever the skeptic, aren't you? Victoria mostly. What?"

"Nothing. I didn't say anything."

"You know I grew up in Victoria."

"Yes, but I didn't know you were a lifeguard."

"Well, now you do. I also worked one summer in Vancouver and another up on the Sunshine Coast." Carol raised her eyebrows but didn't comment again.

Martin knew her entire spotty work history. She'd found a string of temporary jobs after her Mum kicked her out on her eighteenth birthday (while her father looked on helplessly, although he did manage to slip her a small wad of fivers as she was leaving). She'd been a waitress, pizza chef, hotel chambermaid, Line-Dancing

Chicken at an amusement park, bouncing from one futureless job to the next right through her twenties. She had met Martin, a Canadian who was working in the UK on an ancestry visa, during her stint as the Line-Dancing Chicken and, in fact, while she was actually in costume, which made for a pretty good "how we met" anecdote.

After they'd been going out for a few weeks, Martin had told her he wanted to return to Canada to be near his ageing mother. This was fine with Carol, who wanted to get as far away from hers as she could. It was easier to emigrate if they were married, they were told, and so they opted for a small, spontaneous ceremony in a Scottish registry office with strangers for witnesses.

They moved to Toronto and rented a small one-bedroom apartment downtown, just a few blocks from the university. Martin procured a student loan and returned to school. Unsure of what he really wanted to study, he took a B.Ed. and then a master's and subsequently found that teaching high school geography was his true vocation. Carol took a part-time evening course in video editing and toyed with the idea of doing a journalism degree but never quite got around to applying. She continued to do a variety of jobs, including a brief stint as a museum tour guide, several long days as a film extra and some part-time bar work in a comedy club called Punch Up! She often had to work weekends, which gave her a legitimate reason not to accompany Martin to Mississauga to visit Madame Gagnon, her cantankerous mother-in-law.

One night Carol plucked up the courage to take the stage at Punch Up!'s weekly Open Mic. Stand-up comedy was something she'd secretly been thinking about doing for years. She was very nervous and drank quite a lot of beer while waiting for her turn. By the time she got on stage, she felt relaxed and confident. She bombed spectacularly – the people of Toronto, though they claimed to appreciate British comedy, seemed to find her delivery too caustic (at least that was the explanation offered afterwards by a supportive fellow comic with spiky hair and a loud waistcoat). Carol had been so humiliated by the experience that she couldn't even face returning to work behind the bar. This was one of the few things about her that Martin didn't know – he was so used to her impulsively taking and leaving jobs that when she told him she'd quit the comedy club bar, he hadn't even bothered to ask why.

After that, she'd managed to fake her ability to type and use a computer enough to find office temp work, which she hated and was terrible at. It had been a relief when she found out she was pregnant with their first baby and had no choice but accept the full-time position of Mother.

Abby was digging a large hole. Charlie was playing with his sister's shell collection, bashing two together like cymbals, then flinging them down. He picked up a conch shell as if it were a telephone, no doubt mimicking his older sister who had earlier held it to her ear and tried to hear the sound of the ocean but found she couldn't due to the sound of the actual ocean, which was breaking noisily just a few metres away.

"Hewo," said Charlie very seriously. "Hewo dare." Carol smiled.

"Hello, darling," she said. "Are you talking on the phone?"

"Well, shall we move along a bit, then, or what?" said Martin.

"If you're a trained lifeguard, there's no real need, is there?" said Carol.

"Fine. I'm going to go get the boogie boards from the car," said Martin. "I feel like giving it a try. Do you want anything?"

"Just the boogie boards," said Carol. "I fancy giving it a try too."

"Really?"

"Yes really. Why shouldn't I?" Martin shrugged, got up and started to walk barefoot back along the beach towards the distant parking lot.

"Aren't you going to wear your beach shoes?" Carol called after him. Without looking back he lifted his hand and waved at her dismissively. She watched him stumble over a clump of seaweed and realized she was smiling.

"I've made a swimming pool," said Abby, flinging down her shovel and jumping into the hole she'd just dug. Once sitting inside it, she added, "Or maybe it's just a bath." Carol was pleased to note that Abby still pronounced it "barth." Or, rather, "barf." Even though she had been born and raised entirely in North America and had a Canadian father, she had picked up her mother's British accent. Carol knew it wouldn't last long once Abby started big school in the fall, but for now people were always commenting on it, telling them both how "cute" it was, which annoyed Carol, firstly because the word *cute* was annoying, and secondly because the comments were starting to make Abby self-conscious. Just the other day, the poor little girl had asked pointedly for a "glairce of waa-der" instead of her usual, proper "glarse of waw-ter."

Carol looked back along the beach, in the direction Martin had walked, shielding her eyes from the sun and squinting, but she could no longer see her husband. She felt suddenly and unexpectedly bereft.

Last month, they had dropped Charlie off at Abby's daycare for the first time. It was a trial day in preparation for the fall when he was registered to start going three days a week, enabling Carol to return to work part-time.

Charlie was excited about going – he'd been dropping Abby off at the daycare since he was a newborn, and always whined or screamed when it was time to leave. Nevertheless, Carol knew that he was bound to go through some separation anxiety, just as Abby had done when she first started going there two years before. So Carol and Martin had suggested that the children go to the window (the daycare was on the first floor with a clear view of the street below) and wave to their parents from there, while she and Martin would wave back and blow happy kisses. That way, Charlie would understand they had really gone but would be spared the agony of a last poignant hug with Mummy.

The daycare staff had been very understanding, lavishing Charlie with attention when he arrived. Abby had been wonderful too – the perfect big sister. As Carol and Martin left, Abby took Charlie's hand and led him to the window where they climbed onto a stool and stood, peering out, preparing to wave goodbye to their parents.

On the way out of the building Martin's cellphone had rung – some kind of emergency at the school he said – and he had raced ahead to take the call in the quiet of the car. Another father had brushed past Carol, knocking her handbag (which was actually a fairly stylish black diaper bag) from her shoulder. He had apologized, picked it up and introduced himself as Dave, father of Claudia. He had held Carol's hand a fraction longer than necessary and she had noticed the warmth and humour in his brown eyes, had guessed he was probably a bit younger than her, thirty-six or -seven perhaps?

"I'm Carol," she had said. "Mother of Abby. And Charlie, that's my baby, well not really any more – he's in for the first time today."

"Oh wow," Dave had said. "How did the drop-off go?"

"So far so good."

"Fingers crossed."

"Yes," she had said, crossing hers tightly. "Well, nice to meet you, Dave."

"You too, Carol. By the way, sorry to throw this at you, but...would you be at all interested in joining the Board?"

"The Board? Of the daycare, you mean?"

"Yes," said Dave. "I somehow got voted in as Vice-President, and someone just quit, so we're recruiting. You're exactly the type of parent we could use."

"Oh?" said Carol. "And what type is that exactly?"

"Intelligent, good sense of humour, able to read. Most importantly, willing to show up once a month and try to stay awake for two hours," said Dave, definitely flirting, at least a little. Carol smiled, but not flirtatiously. She wished their marriage therapist could see her now – last session he'd had the nerve to suggest that one of

Carol's Recurring Issues was Inappropriate Flirtation.

"Daddy, come on!" Claudia was tugging at her father's jacket.

"Okay, sweetheart," Dave had said, allowing her to drag him away. "Think about it!" he had shouted after Carol.

"Okay, thanks, I will!" Carol shouted back.

She exited the building and saw Martin sitting in the passenger seat, still on his cellphone, glaring at her and pointing agitatedly at his watch. She glanced at her own watch – it was much later than she'd realized, five past eight already. She ran to the car, jumped in and buckled up. Martin shut his cellphone and looked at her.

"Well what are you waiting for?" he said. "I'm going to be late for school."

"We can still do it," she said, starting the car.

They'd been driving a couple of minutes when she suddenly remembered the children. It was like a cold fist had clutched her heart. She'd forgotten to wave at them. She'd forgotten to blow kisses. She'd been so preoccupied with Dave and then with Martin being late – his glowering face – that she hadn't even looked up. She had a vision of them at the window, cherubic faces pressed against the glass, little hands poised to wave, waiting for her – their mother – to look up and see them. Watching as she got in the car and drove away without giving them so much as a glance.

"Oh God!" she cried.

"What?" said Martin. "What's happened?" Tears had sprung to her eyes but she had to keep driving, so she wiped them away angrily.

"Oh Martin, it's the children," she said. "We forgot to wave. Oh my God, they'll be devastated. Jesus, on Charlie's first day! How could we? I'm going to turn around and go back."

"You can't," Martin had said. "If you do that I'll be late for sure."

"What's more important, Martin? Your job or your children?"

"It's the only job we have right now and you know I can't let my students down."

"Right. Of course. So your students do come first."

"Not fair Carol. Look, go back if you like, but you need to drop me first. Besides, there's no easy way to turn around here, so it'll be five or ten minutes before you could get back, by which time you might as well have dropped me."

"Oh, Martin, we're the worst parents in the world!"

"Speak for yourself. Don't worry about it too much. I'll bet they've forgotten about it already and are playing happily."

"Or they're still at the window now, waiting for us to come back and wave and blow kisses like we promised."

"They may not even have bothered waiting at the window. You know how distractible they are. As soon as we left, I'll bet the educators put out some cool toys and they started playing instead."

"You think?" Carol said doubtfully, wanting to believe him.

"I do," said Martin. "And even if they did stay at the window for a moment, it's no big deal – so they got to watch their parents drive away together. It's hardly a tragedy, is it? Trust me, by the time you pick them up this afternoon, they won't even remember the drop-off. I mean, come on, they'll both have had a really full exciting day with a big nap in the middle."

"I suppose that's true," said Carol. "And I suppose if I went back now it might make the separation worse for Charlie."

"Atta girl," said Martin. "They'll be just fine, you'll see."

"Well, I hope you're right," said Carol, deciding to believe him, though for the rest of the day she kept thinking about their sad little faces pressed against the glass.

At three-thirty, Carol entered the daycare centre with some trepidation. Charlie saw her first and came hurtling towards her, yelling "Mama!" in a joyful tone. He flung himself at her legs and she pulled him into a tight embrace. Abby trotted over and joined the hug.

"Did you have a lovely day?" said Carol. "I want to hear all about it." Abby pulled away and looked up at her mother.

"Why didn't you wave at us this morning?" she said.

"Oh God," said Carol, and the cold fist was back, grabbing her useless heart and wringing it. "I'm so sorry. You know Mummy loves you both very much, right?"

"Right. Why didn't you even look at us?" said Abby.

"I know I promised. Did you and Charlie both watch from the window, then?"

"Yes," said Abby. "Just like you told us to. We was waving and waving and waving, Mummy. Why didn't you wave back?"

"I'm so sorry," said Carol miserably. "I was...distracted by...something important and...

Daddy was going to be late and....I'm just so sorry." Charlie was still hugging her tight. She looked down at him and stroked the top of his head.

"Did you have a lovely first day, Charlie?" she said.

"I's cried mummy," said Charlie, turning his little face up towards her. "I's cried and cried."

"Did he really?" Carol asked Abby.

"Quite a bit," said Abby.

By the time Martin returned with the boogie boards, Carol had changed Charlie's diaper twice and was now helping Abby to build a sandcastle city faster than her little brother could knock it down.

"What took you so long?" said Carol to Martin's shadow, lifting the bucket to reveal a perfectly formed castle.

"We're parked at least half a mile away, Carol, and the sand is getting hot."

"I know. That's why I suggested you wore your beach shoes. But you know best."

Martin dropped the boogie boards on the sand.

"You're too tired to try it now, I suppose?" said Carol.

"No," said Martin. "It'll feel good to cool off."

"Well be careful. Remember that riptide. And your age. And the fact you've never tried boogie boarding before. Or have you? Perhaps you're a boogie boarding champion, and you just never got around to mentioning it."

Martin didn't respond, just picked up the larger of the two boards and ran into the shallow surf.

"Where's Daddy going?" asked Abby.

"Boogie boarding," said Carol. "It's supposed to be fun."

"Can I go with him?"

"*May* I go with him? No, it's too dangerous for little children," said Carol. "The water's shallow but the surf is strong. It's just for grown-ups and very big children, sweetie."

"Charlie done poo-poop!" said Charlie. "Poopoopoopoop."

"Oh, come on," said Carol. "Not again." But even in the open air she could smell that her son needed another diaper change. For the umpteenth time, she marvelled at Martin's uncanny knack of avoiding ninety per cent of the nappy changes.

She glanced out into the surf and saw her husband, one of several boogie boarders, lying on his tummy on the sky blue board, gliding into shore on a low-riding wave. She watched him leap to his feet, shake off the water and run back in again, splashing with abandon. He looked really happy. She felt a pang of envy, then guilt. She should have told him by now that she was pregnant again, but she wanted to wait until she was sure. Not until she was sure that she was pregnant – there was no doubt about that. She knew there was no such thing as a false positive and she'd peed on three predictor sticks, each giving a differently presented but definitive "yes" – no, she wanted to wait until she was sure about what she wanted to do.

"Mama poo!" Charlie was already lying down obediently on the beach mat, chubby legs waving in the air, waiting for Carol to change him again.

Just then a family of five marched past – mother, father and three boys in descending order of height. They were all wearing the same, presumably self-imposed, uniform – yellow baseball caps, orange T-shirts with black lettering on the front and back, checkered pink and red seersucker shorts, white sports socks and sneakers. As they passed by, Carol speed-read the words emblazoned on the T-shirts – "DAD" shouted the leader's T-shirt, front and back, followed by "MOM," "KYLE," "KALUM" and "KRIS." Below each name was printed, in slightly smaller font, the same two words: "TEAM HICKS."

"Off," said Charlie. She looked down and saw that he had managed to undo the tabs and was about to remove the soiled diaper himself. She grabbed his hands just in time.

When Martin returned, at least half an hour later, he looked exhilarated.

"Whoa, that was awesome," he said.

"Dude?" said Carol, and Martin smiled.

"Dude," he said, putting on a surfer-boy voice. "Totally. Yeah, that was awesome, dude." Carol found herself smiling back.

"Well good," she said. "Now it's my turn to try. I'm looking forward to it."

"Have fun," he said. "Don't go in too deep – it's a very gradual decline for some way, but then there's a steep drop-off where the water turns a darker blue, see?"

"Yes, I'd already noticed that," said Carol. "I'm not going out nearly that far."

"Okay. So the trick is to wait for a decent wave and to position the board so it's ready to sit right on the crest, then when you feel it coming, you —"

"All right, all right. Thank you, Mr. Instant Expert Surfboarder," said Carol. "I'm sure I'll work it out."

"I'm only trying to give you the benefit of my thirty minutes of experience," said Martin, smiling again. He seemed to be in a better mood than she'd seen him in months.

"Don't take your eyes off the kids," said Carol. "Oh, and Charlie has a touch of diarrhea, so you might have to change him again."

As she removed her baggy T-shirt, Carol sucked in her stomach, which, glancing down, didn't seem to make any difference at all. She was still carrying over twenty pounds of excess baby weight. Quite a bit over twenty – she was, to be exact, forty-seven pounds heavier than her prebaby self. Tucking the smaller boogie board, which was bright red, under her right arm, Carol walked out towards the half-dozen or so other boogie boarders who were squatting in the shallow surf. With her free hand she tugged at her new one-piece bathing suit – it was riding further up her hips than she felt comfortable with. She tried not to look as self-conscious as she felt. The new bathing suit was a change from her usual all-black ones. It was navy blue and covered with small white flowers, with plenty of ruching around the bust and waist. "Flattering" and "slimming" were what the saleswoman kept calling it when Carol had emerged uncertainly from the changing rooms. Right now she regretted having listened to the stupid shop lady's spiel – she was well outside her comfort zone and nothing is more flattering than all-black. She tried to find solace in the fact that Martin had not seemed to notice it.

She reached the other boogie boarders and stopped, glad that she was now visible only from the waist up, not that anyone was looking at her. They all had their boards poised and were facing the beach but with their heads turned back, watching for the swell of the ocean behind them. She copied them, arms outstretched, gripping the front of the board with both hands, holding it out firmly, strap looped around her wrist. She craned her neck to watch for an incoming wave, and noticed that there were a few windsurfers and sailboats out on the water, and a large trawler near the horizon.

She watched and waited for the wave to rise up and carry her in to shore. Her feet were flat on the ocean floor, but her body swayed with the current. She felt a rush of adrenalin as the water rose up a few metres behind and rolled towards her. She turned her head to shore and readied herself, leaning onto the board, but she must not have been far enough out because the wave broke just before it reached her, forcing her into the surf instead of carrying her along on top of it. She was plunged into the crashing foam, spluttering for air and trying to get back on her feet. She'd breathed seawater up her nose; she blew and spat it out. The back of her throat stung and her nostrils ached. At last she was able to stand up. The swirling water came to just above her knees. She pushed back her soggy hair and looked around.

None of the other boarders seemed to have had any trouble. A girl in a teeny bikini glided gracefully by, her sparkling purple boogie board borne aloft by a classically formed whitecap, which bowed into the shallows, setting the teenager down gently.

Carol looked over at her family. Martin was busy playing with the kids; it looked like he was digging a moat around a cluster of sandcastles. Nobody was watching her.

She grabbed the board and headed back out again, determined this time to position herself just right. But again she must have misjudged the wave, again she was too far in when it crested and this time she was slammed onto the seabed, and when she'd struggled to her feet she realized she'd scraped her knee on some rocks or shell. The pain triggered a rush of rage.

"Fuck!" She stood at the water's edge and looked at the injury. It was just a graze and the salt water was, she knew, the best thing for it. She was about to give up and go back to building sandcastles and changing diapers, but then she remembered how Martin had returned all refreshed and happy and calm, his usual tetchiness erased, and she decided to give boogie boarding one last try – third time lucky, she decided.

This time, she made sure that she was level with the other boogie boarders, and then took one more step out so that she would be certain to catch the wave. She readied herself, watching the ocean rise behind her. She felt herself being swept up by the wave and this time had the euphoric feeling she'd been hoping for.

It was, however, short lived. Instead of riding *on* the wave, she suddenly found herself riding *in* it – she was again beneath the surface, gasping for air. She held her breath, clung to the board and tried to remain level, thinking it must be some spray overhead. Sure enough, she quickly surfaced, but she didn't seem any closer to shore. In fact she seemed to have somehow gone backwards. She stretched out her legs to stand but couldn't feel the bottom. Trying not to panic, she trod water and looked around.

It was less noisy than it had been further in, the roar of the ocean breeze and crashing waves was a bit muted and the water was unmistakably darker. She'd somehow gone beyond the drop-off point, but not that much past it – she could see the lighter blue just a few metres in front of her. And there was a man – another boogie boarder – standing, waiting for the next wave, no more than ten or so feet away from her. She was about to yell to him for help, but something stopped her. She was being silly. She could swim the ten feet easily and the current would help –

she would no doubt be carried in by the swell. Why involve a stranger for nothing? It would only serve to embarrass her – she could just see Martin gloating when the man came over afterwards and asked if she was okay.

She held the board in front of her and started to kick with her legs. Almost at once she realized she wasn't moving – or rather, she was moving, but the wrong way. Then she realized that the swell was not happening behind her any more – the closest breakers were now quite some distance in front of her. She would have to call for help after all. But as she opened her mouth, the man caught the wave and boarded away into shore.

"Help!" Carol shouted. But nobody else was anywhere close to being in earshot anymore. Besides, her voice sounded thin and reedy out here beyond the breakers, despite the water's being so much calmer and quieter.

She could still see the shore but could no longer make out individual people. She wondered when Martin or the children would notice she hadn't returned and start looking for her. She tried to locate the nearest lifeguard tower. It seemed to be quite a way down the beach. She regretted not having agreed to move along now. She wondered if she should let go of the boogie board and try to swim, but she was not a very strong swimmer. Also, the board was bright red, which might be helpful if there happened to be a coastguard helicopter in the vicinity. Also, it belonged to the people whose condo they were renting and she didn't know where to buy an exact replacement.

One thing Carol decided she'd try to do was to keep facing the shore. It was bad enough that she was drifting out to sea alarmingly fast, but pointing the wrong way would somehow make it worse, as if she were deliberately hastening her departure. Then again, she wondered if her best hope was to be picked up by one of the sailboats she'd seen earlier, or even hauled up onto the giant, rusty trawler on the horizon by some burly eastern Europeans.

She knew how ridiculous it would be to die this way, while trying to boogie board for the first time. She was suddenly struck by the irony of what good material this would make were she ever to attempt stand-up comedy again. The punchline would be something to do with her untimely death and the boogie board. Death and the boogie board. It sounded a little bit like the title of a surreal but comic play. Something else she'd always wanted to try was writing. Perhaps if she lived she would write a brilliant surreal but comic play. Perhaps she'd start a blog.

What the hell was wrong with her? How could she be thinking about hypothetical stand-up routines and blogging at a time like this? This was terrifying. She was a mother.

She tried to picture Abby and Charlie happily building sandcastles, probably still unaware of their mother's plight, and was surprised that she didn't start crying or feeling more panicky. Or was she, in fact, panicking right now? Were her thoughts so jumbled and astonishingly trivial for a reason? Were her thoughts trying to stave off tragedy? She wondered if she should try praying, even though she didn't really believe in God. Perhaps if she prayed and then survived she would become a born-again Christian and grow bangs and home-school her children and make everyone wear frumpy, handmade clothing.

Of course, if she were a born-again Christian, there would be no question about keeping the baby. Not only that, but she would probably want to have more than just three children. She would probably keep on having babies until menopause struck or her breasts hit the floor, whichever happened first, and the only way to pay for everything was to get a reality TV series.

She was probably about six weeks along by now. Perhaps that was why she wasn't panicking – her hormones were making her calm and reasonable. She and Martin had talked about trying for a third child just in order to stave off her PMS for another eighteen months or so. Or perhaps this was a test. If she lived, it would be because of the baby. It was meant to be. It was a special baby who would one day save the world. Or it was a chance to redeem herself and prove she could be a good mother who didn't forget to wave at her children. Or perhaps the trauma was going to induce a miscarriage, and she'd be spared the decision altogether, and Charlie would be spared the fate of being a middle child, and their nicely balanced family dynamic would not be upset. Then she would probably spend the rest of her life feeling guilty and grief-stricken and wondering if it had been a boy or a girl.

She thought about Martin and how badly they'd been getting on lately and vowed that she would stop winding him up – if she lived, obviously – stop pressing his buttons, stop engaging in petty bickering and try really hard to make him happy. She still loved him, after all, didn't she? Of course she did. And he still loved her, she was pretty sure.

She knew now that she had to tell him she was pregnant, and as soon as possible – that is if she made it back to shore alive. If she drowned, they would no doubt cut her open and discover the fetus. And later, when the shock and grief began to subside, Martin would wonder if she'd known and, if so, why she hadn't told him.

Carol realized that if deciding to keep the baby would guarantee she got to live, she would gladly decide to keep it. She also realized this wasn't quite the same as truly wanting to keep it.

She had drifted out another thirty feet at least, maybe more. She had also moved along the shore quite a bit and wondered if she would soon find herself parallel to the military beach and whether that would make her situation more or less dangerous. She aimed the board's nose towards the receding coastline and kicked her legs vigorously, but it was no use, she could feel she was still moving gently backwards.

It was so much calmer out here, and colder. She suddenly thought about the sea creatures that might be circling below her. She instinctively pulled her legs up and craned her neck slightly, hoping to catch sight of a yacht behind her, or a dinghy. All she could see was the trawler, anchored on the horizon, still quite a distance away, but now close enough for her to see how very large and very rusty it was.

She strained her ears, hoping for the sound of a human voice, or a motor. All she could hear was the lapping of the water and the shrieking of gulls overhead. *I really am going to die out here*, thought Carol, and suddenly the only thing she was aware of was that she ached to be with her family.

A figure burst into sight, swimming rapidly towards her through the waves. At first Carol thought she must be hallucinating. The swimmer reached her quite quickly, and she saw that it was a young man, mid-twenties at most, with dark, closely cropped hair, a deep tan and a red floatation device. He stopped swimming just a couple of metres away from her.

"You're too far out," he said.

"Yeah, I know," she replied.

"Are you in trouble?" he said, probably thrown by her bizarrely conversational tone.

"Oh yes, I'm in trouble," said Carol, coming to her senses. "Thanks for coming out. That is if you did. Did you? Are you a lifeguard? Are you here to rescue me?"

"Yes," he said and swam over to her. "Hold on to this." Carol did as she was told, but it was not easy to grasp the fat little floatie. Then she saw that it had slats. She grabbed hold and looked at her rescuer, who was winding the floatie's string around his wrist.

"Can you swim?" he asked.

"A little," she said. "Is it okay to keep the boogie board too? It's not really mine."

"We'll see," he said.

"I don't make a habit of this, by the way. It was my first time boogie boarding. First and last," she said, forcing a laugh.

"You got caught in the rip," he said. "Didn't you hear the announcements?"

"Oh," she said.

"Hold on tight to the floatation device, and I'm going to support you like this. I need to swim us in and the current's pretty strong today."

She obeyed the instructions and felt his arm tighten around her sternum. Then he started to swim. He was an incredibly strong swimmer, but it couldn't have been easy. She tried to swim too – kicking a little, while attempting to transform herself into a light load for him, but she could feel she was dragging him down. Still, he kept going and already they had made good progress.

He paused for a moment and looked her in the eye. "What's your name?" he said.

"Carol," she said. "What's yours?"

"Last name?" he said.

"Cope. Cope-Gagnon."

"Married?"

"'Fraid so," she said, with a little smile.

"Where do you live?".

"Toronto," she said, adding, "that's in Canada."

"How old are you?"

"Just turned forty-one," she said, realizing she was probably old enough to be his mother. Or at least his much older sister. "Why are you asking?"

"It's routine," he said. "I have to write up an incident report afterwards."

"Oh, I see. Of course. Have there been many other people needing rescuing today?"

"Yes," he said. "It's the riptide."

"Right," she said.

They didn't speak after that. Carol concentrated her energy into holding onto the floatation device and keeping her head above water while her young rescuer swam endlessly against the current, cutting through the surf towards the shore. She could now make out the faces of people on the beach and saw that quite a large crowd seemed to have gathered at the water's edge. Then she noticed flashing lights, which were on top of some kind of van. It looked like an emergency vehicle and she wondered what had happened, then realized that what had happened was her.

They at last reached the shallower water, safely on the other side of the breakers, and the ocean was no longer working against them. There were still a few boogie boarders waiting for the waves or skimming along, seemingly oblivious to the danger they were in. At last her feet touched the bottom, but the lifeguard still had hold of her and she felt obliged to go along with whatever he wanted, so she kept holding on to the floatie and half-swimming, until the water was so shallow she was crawling on all fours.

The lifeguard stood up and held out his hand. She grasped it and he pulled her to her feet. She handed him back his flotation device.

"Thank you again," she said. "Really, I can't thank you enough."

"No problem, Ma'am," he said. "It's my job." And with that, he ran off towards the lifeguard tower.

Carol picked up the boogie board, which had miraculously stayed attached to her wrist. Then she started scanning the beach, trying to get her bearings and locate her family. She knew she'd drifted quite a way along the shore – luckily so, as that's presumably how the lifeguard had been able to spot her.

"Carol! Carol!" Martin was running towards her, holding Charlie, with Abby scampering behind him.

"Where have you been?" he said. "You've been gone over half an hour."

"Is that all?" she said, surprised.

"What happened?" he said. "I was getting worried. I saw the flashing lights and people looking out to sea and someone said a swimmer was drowning. Then I tried to spot you and couldn't. How come you're this far along the shore? Are you okay?"

"I'm fine," she said. "Ready for a rest now, though."

"Come and see what we made, Mummy," said Abby. "It's got shops and moats and everything!"

They walked back to their spot in silence, Martin carrying Charlie and the boogie board, Carol holding her daughter's hand until Abby broke away and ran ahead excitedly.

"Look, Mummy!" she cried. Carol gave the sandcastle city two thumbs up.

The sun was high in the sky now. Carol was shivering. She sank down onto the beach mat and pulled a towel around her shoulders.

She looked over at her husband. He had just finished changing Charlie's diaper and was re-membering to reapply sunscreen. Charlie tod-dled off to join his sister. Martin came over and sat down next to Carol.

"So, how did you like the boogie boarding? Pretty amazing, huh?"

"Oh yes," she said. "It was great."

TALL FOOD

"What's *with* all the tall food?"

Ellie chuckled appreciatively. Her boyfriend Rob was always saying witty things, making her laugh. The oversized book-style menu had reclaimed his attention.

"I mean," he continued, "who decided that stacking it up makes it taste better? If it's laid out nice and flat, you know exactly what you're getting *and* it's cheaper. When they pile it all up and give it fancy names it suddenly costs a fortune and you can't even know for sure what the fuck is in there!" She'd winced at the profanity; she preferred it when he kept his joking clean, but she wasn't yet comfortable enough with him to say anything. She wanted to but had decided to wait until they were at least engaged. This was, after all, only their second date.

"I mean, seriously," said Rob. He read the menu aloud, slowly and derisively: "*Blackened red snapper with reduction of balsamic bumbleberry coulis...*" He broke off with a snort.

Ellie tried not to let her disappointment show. She had been leaning towards the *Blackened red snapper with reduction of balsamic bumbleberry coulis, flame-broiled baby market vegetables and roasted garlic mashed yam with nutmeg shavings*. Now that he'd mocked it she'd have to go with something else. She had a sudden image of their wedding reception dinner, tall food everywhere, and a cake in the centre, its forty layers stretching into the rafters. For some reason, the image made her smile. Rob smiled too.

"At least the fad for sun-drying seems to have passed," he said.

"How do you mean?"

"Remember when everything was sun-dried? It started with tomatoes. Then it spread to apricots and mangoes. Pretty soon everything was sun-dried!"

"Except maybe chicken?"

"Well, I guess not chicken."

On their first date last week (before it had been cut short by a waiter spilling soup all over Rob – thankfully, it had been cold soup, vichyssoise) Rob had explained that delivery was everything when it came to jokes – you had to have good timing. She'd never been much good at telling jokes. She couldn't get the rhythm right, and also had a hard time remembering punchlines. She guessed she took after her mother that way, although, like her mother, she had always been really good at appreciating comedy.

Her parents had met while crossing the Atlantic on the QE2 steamship from Portsmouth to New York City in 1976. As her mother often said, "Your dad was funnier than the ship's hired entertainment. Had me in stitches the whole way across." They had quickly discovered that they were both emigrating to Canada. Three months later they were married and settling into life in Hamilton, Ontario. Three years after that, Ellie was born, and soon her dad was making both his girls laugh on a daily basis.

He was especially good at pranks, her dad. Every couple of months, since she was six or seven years old, Ellie would find he'd made her an "apple pie bed." This meant that although the bed looked normal, when she tried to get into it, her feet would hit a solid wall of sheet a metre or so down.

"Ha ha, Dad! Good one!" she would call down the stairs before stripping off the blankets and sheets and remaking the bed so that she could get in and sleep. Even now she would never get into bed without first plunging her arm in to investigate.

That's probably why a good sense of humour was second (after decent personal hygiene) on Ellie's top five list of attributes she was looking for in a potential life partner slash husband.

"What are you having?" she asked Rob. "Have you decided?"

"Definitely not the soup," he said, and they both smiled. "No, all I want is something that doesn't resemble a skyscraper. Is that too much to ask?"

"What about pizza?" she said. "Would that be flat enough for you?" He didn't reply, but she noticed his smile fading; he looked down at the menu and frowned. She wondered if she'd inadvertently hit a nerve. Perhaps he'd had some unfortunate incident involving a pizza that she didn't know about. She hoped she hadn't said something that would stop him asking her on a third date.

It had been a long time since she'd been on a third date with anyone, and a really long time since she'd been on a fourth. It had, in fact, been seventeen years, and she still remembered every painful detail.

She'd walked home from school with Kevin Fletcher three days in a row. They barely spoke, but she felt comfortable in his company and it seemed to be mutual. On the fourth day, Melissa Tomkins had pulled her aside in the girls' locker room and told her that today Kevin would be expecting a kiss from Ellie when they parted ways, a proper kiss, and by "proper," Melissa had said, she meant "French." Ellie didn't know what that was, but luckily Melissa's advice was very specific – she told Ellie that when it was time to say goodbye to Kevin she should stand still, tilt her head to one side, close her eyes and stick her tongue out. Ellie had done exactly as Melissa advised, but instead of meeting her outstretched tongue, Kevin had said, "What are you, some kind of retard?" and she'd opened her eyes to see him laughing and pointing at her maniacally as he backed away.

The following day all his friends had asked

her to show them how to perform freaky tongue kisses and had started calling her "Frenchie." Even her own friends, like Melissa, had stopped speaking to her.

She had had a few third dates over the years but was often the only one who showed up for them. Sometimes the guy called to cancel, sometimes he didn't. She'd read in a magazine article about dating rules that you're supposed to have sex right after the third date. Or was it right before? No, she was pretty sure it was right after. She'd also read, in another article in another magazine, that guys sometimes got anxious in anticipation of sexual intercourse and that this had something to do with fear of performance, but she couldn't quite understand what that meant.

Of course she got that it was referring to the sex itself, but she had had sex twice and there had been no performing at all, either by her or the guy. But maybe that's because he hadn't been the right guy, the one she was destined to be with forever. Maybe when she met her true life partner slash husband there would, in fact, be a performance. She held out secret hope that it would be something to do with poetry recitation, though not necessarily the kind that rhymed, which she had loved in her naïve youth but which now, at thirty-one, she more often than not found trite.

She scanned the menu again, but nothing appealed as much as the red snapper. She had recently taken a two-day assertiveness workshop in which she had learned to scream freely in a circle of women and state her needs without shame or fear of reprisal.

"I am, in fact, going to have the red snapper," she said firmly, closing the menu and placing it on the table. She smiled faintly and looked at Rob, expecting him to say something sarcastic about the height of her chosen dish, but he didn't. He didn't even look up. He continued to look at the menu. He had exceptionally long eyelashes.

"Have you decided yet?" she said after a while.

"Well," he said at last, and his tone, to her delight, was once again lighthearted and playful. "I am now, thanks for pointing it out, seriously considering the pizza and —"

"Let me guess," she said. "Thin crust! Right? Because that way it'll be super low! Because a deep dish one could rise up and be tall, or at least not be totally flat? So thin crust pizza! Am

I right?" He didn't respond, other than to frown at the menu again.

She wondered if her own display of decisiveness had somehow affected him negatively. She'd been reading about power dynamics in relationships and how some marriages can suffer from a deadly recurring syndrome called "Me Up, You Down." But perhaps it didn't apply since they weren't yet married. She hoped he would choose soon and start being funny again. She was really hungry and starting to feel a little bit sad. His eyes were darting all over the menu. She felt sorry for him; he clearly had a problem with indecision. She decided to try and help him out.

"How about sharing a side salad?" she said. "They're not too tall, are they?"

"All right, all right," he said.

"Okay, great. So what would you prefer? Green or Caesar? Or Greek?"

"Whatever." He looked bored now, or perhaps he was really angry about something. If there was one thing she'd learned about guys, it was that they got angry sometimes out of the blue about goodness knows what but didn't come out and tell you what it was about. Men were complicated. She'd learned not to take it personally.

"I think I'd prefer the Greek," she said at last. "Would you?"

"Sure, I guess," he said.

"Really? Me too!" This was the third like or dislike they'd found they shared so far. She made a mental check mark.

"Are we getting wine?" she asked.

"I don't think that's a good idea, do you?" he said, and beckoned to the waiter. Ellie was quite relieved, as white wine usually gave her a headache, while red wine tended to turn her lips black. This had only served her well on one occasion – the day she and her guinea pig had entered an owner/pet look-alike contest (they'd received an honourable mention). The waiter came, took their order and cleared away their wineglasses.

"I just need to go check on my elephant," said Rob, and she laughed, a little too loudly perhaps, but she wanted to be sure to give him positive feedback and encourage him to continue being funny for her. He'd said, "I just need to go check on my elephant" on their first date last week, and she'd been totally confused and hadn't known she should laugh. Then, when he'd come back from the washroom, he'd explained it was something called a "euphemism" and then explained why it was hilarious, and then she'd understood, but it was a bit too late to laugh, so she was making up for it now.

Rob stood up, pushing his chair back as he did so. It made a scraping sound on the terracotta-tiled floor and she flinched. He was much taller than he looked when sitting, indicating a truncated body, which she wanted to ask him about but decided to wait until later. She was quite short herself – 5'2", which was too short to be a policewoman, someone had once told her. That same person – her aunt Flo, an imposing 5'10" – had also told her that tall men shouldn't be allowed to date short women because it was a despicable waste of a tall man. Yet after two brief affairs with major league basketball players, Aunt Flo had eloped with a 5'4" carpenter who encouraged her to wear stilettos at all times. They subsequently settled in Boise, Idaho, and Ellie rarely saw them.

"Won't be long," said Rob, and he opened the washroom door, which was just beyond their table. The door opened outwards, and in place of the word *Gents* or the classic men's room icon was a laminated picture of Luciano Pavarotti. She wondered if they'd change it now that he was dead, or if it was his dying that had prompted them to use it. Rob disappeared into the washroom and so did Pavarotti's frozen expression of pained ecstasy – eyebrows atilt, mouth open. Ellie wondered whose picture they had chosen to stick on the women's washroom door. She couldn't think of the names of any female Italian opera singers.

The restaurant was filling up, the noise level rising steadily. The chatter of patrons and clatter of cutlery on plates now almost drowned out the background music, which alternated between classical and Motown. An elderly man and woman – Ellie guessed them to be late seventies – entered the restaurant to the chorus of "Downtown" and were seated in the bay window at a table for two with a *Reserved* sign on it. The table she and Rob had been given had had a *Reserved* sign on it too, but it was in a busy thoroughfare and, she now knew, very close to the washrooms. Waiters and other patrons kept bumping Ellie's chair and brushing the tablecloth as they passed, making the Chianti bottle-in-a-basket candle holder shudder. She reached out to steady it, and a drop of hot, red wax dripped onto her hand. She waited for it to harden and peeled it slowly from her skin.

The old couple was holding hands and

whispering to one another. Rob returned and sat down.

"Well," he said, looking around. "This is nice."

"Yes," she replied. "It's very nice, isn't it? Have you been here before?"

"No."

"Me neither." She was still watching the older couple but couldn't get her mind off the mystery picture on the women's washroom door. She decided to relieve her curiosity.

"I just have to go check on my yak," she said as she stood up. Rob sort of smiled, but not with his eyes, so perhaps it was only funny if you said "elephant." She walked past Pavarotti until she reached the door of the women's washroom. The picture was of Madonna, from her *Evita* era. Ellie didn't really need to use the washroom, so she returned to their table and found Rob talking on his phone. He was smiling a lot and speaking in the same low voice he'd used when he approached her in the office where she was temping. He was there that day selling ecologically friendly office supplies and had just offered the manager a free assessment of the company's off-gassing ratios. Ellie remembered how he'd stared at her legs when he spoke to her – she was wearing a skirt she'd mistakenly tumble dried on high heat.

When he saw she'd come back, Rob rang off immediately.

"Sorry about that. Work call," he said. "You were quick."

"Yes. I didn't really need to go."

"Oh. Hey, I think our dinner's coming," said Rob. It wasn't – the waitress whooshed past them with two steaming plates intended for someone else. They both lifted their faces and inhaled. For another ten minutes they sat quietly, not speaking. Ellie didn't mind the lack of conversation – it was important to be able to be silent sometimes. At last the Greek salad was deposited between them, but Rob didn't seem to want any after all. Ellie lifted her fork and poked at the salad, managing to secure a cube of cucumber, tomato and feta cheese on each of the three prongs. She glanced at the bay window and noticed that the old couple was sharing a plate of oysters. She chewed the mouthful of salad, enjoying the tang of the dressing. She swallowed.

"It's good," she said. "Sure you don't want some?" Rob shook his head and looked at his phone – a text had come in, presumably more urgent business. He started texting back. Ellie chewed slowly, watching his thumbs move around the miniature keyboard, punching the tiny keys. He was quite dexterous.

Rob's pizza finally arrived with a large sprig of fresh rosemary standing up in the centre like a tree. He plucked it off and put it to the side of his plate without comment. Ellie's red snapper was draped over a hillock of orange mash from which protruded assorted miniature vegetables. It was all surrounded by a dark purple moat.

"Pepper?" asked the waitress, holding up an extraordinarily large wooden pepper mill.

"No thanks," said Ellie.

"I'll have some," said Rob. "I want to watch how you handle such a big one." He winked at the waitress, but she didn't seem to notice. She looked only at his pizza as she ground the massive mill above it, showering his dish with black dots.

"What on earth do you do with that after dark?" said Rob. "Are you allowed to take it home with you?" He grinned and Ellie laughed – what a silly idea! The waitress' expression didn't change. She continued to grind the mill.

"Enough?" she said.

"Not quite. I can take a whole lot of heat, if

you know what I mean," said Rob.

"Okay, say when," said the waitress, and she gave the pepper mill a sudden sharp twist. A black cloud fell onto the centre of Rob's thin-crust pie.

"When!" cried Rob. The waitress stopped grinding and leant the peppermill against her shoulder, elbow crooked, the way a soldier might hold a rifle.

"Anything else?" said the waitress, still looking at Rob's pizza.

"No thanks," said Rob.

"Enjoy your meal," said the waitress, and she walked away.

"What an awesome waitress," said Ellie, and she stabbed a baby gourd. Rob didn't respond. They ate in silence, punctuated by the occasional, "That looks good!" "Is that good?" "Mmmm! It's very good!" "Not too hot?" "No, it's just how I like it." Three times Rob held up his glass for a refill, but their waitress didn't seem to notice him. At last he got the attention of a waiter they'd not seen before, who brought over a pitcher of iced water.

When they'd both finished, the same waiter brought the bill and laid it down in between them. They both looked at it for a while before suddenly reaching for it at the same moment. Their fingertips touched and withdrew. Ellie's tingled for some time afterwards. She felt a deep connection with Rob, on more than one level.

"Shall we go Danish?" she said.

"No, no, I'll get it," he said.

"I'd be happy to split it."

This was a familiar second date scenario – a short back and forth dance then the guy usually paid, then usually failed to show up for the third date. She didn't want that to happen this time. She had a feeling Rob might be "the one." She needed to split the bill.

"No, no, let me get it," said Rob. "It's tax deductible anyway. As long as we talked about work."

"Oh. But we didn't, did we?"

"Didn't we? I thought we had."

"No. I don't think so." Rob pulled a business card from his wallet and handed it to her. It said "Robert J. Winter, President" and underneath was the company's logo, a picture of the Earth ringed by the company's name, *Home and Office Eco-Solutions, Inc.* She wondered what the "J" stood for.

"If you ever want a free assessment of your home, I'd be happy to oblige," he said. "You'd be amazed about the off-gassing from melamine, for instance."

"Seriously? My parents have melamine everywhere," she said.

"Oh, well I'll give you a card for them too then, shall I?" he said.

"It's okay, we can share. I still live with my parents," she said.

"Oh, I see," he said. She looked again at his business card.

"What does the J stand for? No, don't tell me; let me guess. Jonathan?"

"Oh, no. No. I don't really have a middle name. I just thought it scanned better with a middle initial. So I added the 'J'."

"Oh. So it's not Justin, then? That was my next guess. Or Jordan? No wait, I know – is it Jack? Or Junior?"

"No. I honestly don't have a middle name. I made it up."

"Oh. Because it could have been Jeremy, or even John. That's making a comeback, isn't it?"

"So you think your parents could benefit from my services, then?"

"Oh yes, I do."

"Great. So get them to call me, okay? They won't be sorry."

"Okay, I will." This evening was going better than Ellie could have possibly imagined. None of her dates had ever given her a business card before. She pictured the consultation in her parents ecologically challenged kitchen, her mother making them tea and her father asking Rob embarrassing questions about off-gassing and his intentions towards their only child. She felt very excited. Rob would teach her parents about off-gassing, and her parents would be bowled over by their future son-in-law, his knowledge, his dedication to his career and his awesome sense of humour.

The waiter returned with the Visa slip.

"So that was definitely a working dinner," Rob said, with a wink and a smile as he filed the receipt in his wallet. This was wonderful – absolute proof of how very much he liked her. She wanted to reassure him it was mutual, that his romantic love was requited, so she winked back at him, though it was more of a blink because she'd never been able to close one eye independently of the other. She adjusted her dress, tucking the bra strap under the shoulder strap. She hoped her mascara hadn't smudged too badly. Now she regretted not having gone into the washroom to check.

"Thank you for dinner, Rob," she said. "It was very nice."

Rob's phone shuddered and beeped, indicating he had another text message. He glanced at it but this time didn't text back. The poor guy might be something of a workaholic, but that wasn't necessarily a bad thing. He was diligent and committed, exactly the traits a husband needed to have.

"Sorry about that," said Rob. "It never stops."

At the exit, they paused to retrieve their coats from the rack near the front doors. On a marble table was a bowl piled with little white mints. Ellie reached for one.

"I wouldn't if I were you," said Rob. "I read an article about how they analyzed those things and found most of them were covered in piss." Ellie smiled and popped one in her mouth.

"You never stop, do you, Rob? So funny."

"I'm not joking," said Rob. "It's because so many people don't wash their hands after using the bathroom. Disgusting but true, I'm afraid."

"Ha ha, yeah right," she said. He really was about as hilarious as they get, although she didn't totally understand this latest joke of his. Still, no matter. The mint was delicious, smooth and round and sweet and refreshing.

She wondered where their next date would be. Rob would probably try to arrange a third date when he dropped her home. Then she realized it wasn't all that late. Perhaps he was going to suggest they go on somewhere else. She hoped so – this was the best second date she'd ever had and she'd love the evening to continue. Perhaps they'd take a cab somewhere or stroll through the city on foot. She wondered if he'd tell more jokes on the way. She hoped so. She loved to laugh.

TEA LEAVES

When I was six, I spotted what appeared to be a large, green butterfly dying in the gutter. I squatted down for a closer look and saw that it was, in fact, a fluttering one-pound note. I picked it up and showed it excitedly to my mother.

"Right, we'd better hand it in," she said.

"Hand it in?" I wailed. "But I thought it was, 'Finders Keepers, Losers Weepers!'"

"Some poor person lost that money," she said firmly. "And they should be given a chance to reclaim it."

We went straight to the nearest police station. It took a while for the grumpy policeman on duty to fill in all the paperwork, but at last he handed my mother a form to sign and told us that if nobody had claimed it after one month, it was ours. Thirty-one days later we returned, and I was so worried that it had been claimed by its rightful owner – or worse, some impostor – that I didn't speak the whole way there. To my great relief and joy, it had not been claimed, and at last it was mine. I valued that pound note more than anything I've received since, and instead of spending it right away, I waited a good couple of hours to turn it into sweeties.

You could get a lot of candy for one pound back then, especially if you shopped in the penny sweet section. From then on, my five pence a week allowance never quite satisfied me, and gradually my gluttonous cravings ate away at my moral centre, which turned out to be as soft as that of the Pear Drop Surprises I longed for.

At age ten I was caught stealing sweets from a corner newsagent's along with an accomplice, my eight-year-old neighbour Andrew. We'd been nicking candy – chocolate bars, packets of Hubba Bubba and Bubblicious gum, tubes of Refreshers, Spangles and Fruit Pastilles, fistfuls of Drumsticks, bags of Sherbet Dip Dabs and rolls of Sherbet Fountains (even though we hated the liquorice) – for a few days, my little cohort and I, growing steadily more confident, then complacent, as we got away with it so easily. Our looks were in our favour and we knew it – we were a couple of androgynous cherubs, plump-cheeked, wide-eyed, with good manners, pudding-bowl haircuts and hand-knitted cardigans. The adrenalin rush soon dissipated, along with the pleasure. But we couldn't stop. We were careful not to hit the same shop too often, though, trawling the neighbourhood for alternate targets.

The day we were caught, we had become greedy, cocky and reckless. The pockets of our anoraks were already bulging with gum, chews and sucky sweets, but I couldn't resist taking a couple more items and stuffed a Curly Wurly up my jumper, then reached for a tube of Smarties, which I managed to secrete in the elastic waistband of my trousers, confident that the sound of the newsagent's radio would drown out the rattling. I was just taking my inconspicuous leave of the shop – very slowly, doubled over and hugging my whole body – when my head was gripped by a large hand. The shock made my arms shoot up and about half the loot tumbled out over the shop floor.

The terrifying, red-faced shopkeeper gave us a choice: He could call our parents, or the police. We hesitated for a moment, weighing up the pros and cons of each, but he didn't wait for our response. We watched, powerless, as his huge, hairy index finger dialled.

"Hello?" he bellowed into the receiver. "Yes! I want the police. That's right, the *police*..." Then he noticed us at his feet, clawing at his ankles, quaking and begging and sobbing, and he hung up. "All right, now," he said, lifting his leg and trying to shake us off. "I didn't really call the bobbies. I was just giving you a fright. I still had my hand on the doo-dad."

Our parents arrived quickly. They were shocked and saddened and mortifyingly apologetic and paid for everything we'd stolen and made us say sorry to the shopkeeper. That part was easy – we were truly sorry, especially about getting caught.

"That should learn you," said the shopkeeper. "Getting caught in the act was the best thing that could've happened – it'll keep you on the straight and narrow for life."

My illicitly gotten goods had come to a total of forty-nine pence, although later that night I realized the amount should have been a nice round fifty as, when I undressed, a penny chew fell out onto the fitted carpet. I quickly unwrapped and ate it. But the ignominy of that day never left me, and I would shudder with shame whenever I thought of it, which was often. The return of my conscience had apparently halted my juvenile delinquency just in time and I entered adulthood a law-abiding young woman, certain to sin no more.

I'd been working in the clothes shop for about three months when I transgressed. I was nineteen but still looked about ten, which, now that I think of it, might have been a factor.

In 1987, The Peacock Trading Company was a store in transition. Little did we know that in a few years it would shorten its name to Peacock and become one of the trendiest and most successful fashion chains in Britain. But for now, clothes only accounted for about fifty per cent of the stock, while half the shop floor was still devoted to the ethnic ware – handwoven rugs, silver stash boxes, jangling jewellery – that a couple of hippies with business savvy had used to launch the company a decade earlier in the form of a Camden Market stall, hawking the cheap goods they'd smuggled over from India in their backpacks.

Our branch was in Brighton and the biggest of nine dotted around southern England. The large shop area was on ground level, while steps in the centre led down to the basement, which housed a windowless café, a stockroom and a small manager's office. The store was well situated. It straddled a pedestrian-only passageway that meandered away from the quaint cafés and bustling antique shops of the Lanes and a two-way side road that led north to the main high street and south to the seafront. In the summer months the customers were mostly out-of-towners – tourists holidaying by the sea, or day-trippers. But during the school year the clientele was mostly comprised of locals who reflected Brighton's four main (or at least, most visible) demographics: university student, young mum, old lady, gay clubber.

A steady stream of potential shoppers flowed in through the propped-open doors. However, a fair number of them coursed right past the eye-catching window displays, which featured that season's clashing cotton jersey separates stretched over metal-framed mannequins whose heads resembled giant coat hangers and whose wire hands modelled ethnic hardware – here a wicker laundry basket, there a fake bong. I'd recently been promoted to Fashion Supervisor, so the window displays were officially my fault.

I was elated when I learned that I would be receiving a pay raise along with my limited extra duties and elevated job title, though I didn't dare ask how much for fear of seeming rude or pushy. I soon found out – eagerly tearing open my first paycheque after the promotion, I saw that the increase amounted to twenty-two pounds and fifty-three pence a month, after taxes. It wouldn't even cover my ever-burgeoning overdraft fees. My bad habit of being in the black for just two days a month following the deposit of my wages was set to continue.

Luckily I had the friendship and support of my colleagues. We were all in it together – earning a pittance, staving off the boredom with gossip, tea breaks and laughter. We were a disparate group of characters but banded together quickly and intensely. The Branch Manager was Shadia, a twenty-eight-year-old who'd immigrated to England from Iran as a teenager. She still lived with her parents, who were constantly trying (and failing) to arrange a marriage for her. The Assistant Manager, Colin, was a twenty-two-year-old George Michael look-alike – so much so that people were always asking for his autograph, apparently not in the least surprised to find the pop star working in a clothes shop. Whenever anyone suggested that Colin was trying to look like the celebrity, he got huffy.

"It's the other way round, thank you," he would say. "I grew the stubble and got my crucifix earring three months before the first photo of George's new image came out. He must've seen me somewhere and copied my look. I ought to sue him."

The other two Supervisors were Patrick (Ethnic Ware) and Mel (Jewellery). Mel was twenty, a petite Northerner who gave the impression of quiet introversion but actually had a wicked tongue to match her sharp wit. She lived with her partner, Walnut, who picked her up every day at closing time and whose mohawk seemed at odds with his soft-spoken shyness. Patrick was twenty-five, wore faded "Frankie Goes to Hollywood" T-shirts, stonewashed, too-tight jeans and the combination scent of cheap aftershave, imported beer, cigarettes and mouthwash.

Patrick was disarmingly open about his disastrous dating experiences, and quickly became our prime source of entertainment. He was looking for long-term love but settling for short-term. He was quite open about his sexual preferences, and I found his confession that he liked to frequent S&M gay fetish clubs but was too shy to move away from the wall, let alone speak to anyone, endearing. I imagined him standing in the shadows, swigging from his bottle of Sol stopped with a wedge of lime, hoping some kinky part-time sadist would spot him and give him a good seeing-to for being so introverted.

Patrick liked all kinds of leather and bondage but confessed that his biggest sexual fantasy was to be restrained by a man in uniform. And his preferred uniform was that of a policeman. The trouble was, he wanted it to be not only a real copper, but a real, straight copper. This was one of the reasons Patrick was having trouble finding a satisfying relationship.

"I've got a weak spot for breeders," he admitted. "The cops in the clubs are mostly Village People wannabes and frankly, that just don't float my boat. Bom."

He had a Cornish accent and a strange little tic – he finished most sentences with a mysterious utterance that sounded like "bom." It usually served to underline a statement, standing in for a full stop or an exclamation mark. At other times it was an indication of embarrassment or nervousness. And sometimes he said it for no apparent reason.

One day he told us the story of how he'd come out to his parents.

"I was twenty," said Patrick. "I'd been moved out for quite a while by then, and had gone home for a weekend visit. I decided to tell them separately, starting with Mum."

She had apparently embraced him at once and cried, "Oh, Patrick, thank God! You had me worried. I thought you were going to tell me there was something wrong with you." His eyes filled with tears of appreciation on relating this part – he adored his mother and she him.

"Now when she comes and stays with me, we walk along the seafront together checking out the fit boys," he said proudly. "Bom."

His father had not visited him in Brighton and likely never would. Buoyed by such a positive response from his mother, Patrick had decided to just blurt it out to his dad, man to man. He'd forgotten that it was actually gay man to homophobe.

"I realized right away that I'd made a mistake," said Patrick. "I should never have told him while he was driving."

They were motoring along a particularly beautiful part of the rugged Cornish coastline not that far from the family home, but even closer to some very steep cliffs. His father was fiddling with the radio dials, looking for Frank

Sinatra. Having no luck, and fed up with landing on static, he turned it off. After thirty seconds of silence, Patrick decided this was his moment.

"Dad," he said, without preamble. "I'm homosexual." His father said nothing, did not even alter his facial expression, but gradually increased his foot pressure on the accelerator and turned the steering wheel slightly until they were speeding straight towards a precipice.

Patrick shut his eyes and gripped the seat with both hands, terrified. At the last minute, he cried, "Don't forget about Mum!" and his father squealed to a spectacular stop, just a few inches from the edge. Then, at last, he spoke to his only son.

"Don't tell me what to do with your mother!" he said. "And you know what else? We will never, ever, speak of this again. You do what you have to do. I don't need to know about it, or hear about it. Got it?"

"Got it, Dad," said Patrick. "Bom."

Patrick may not have found his life partner yet, but he did manage to have fulfilling one-night stands. One morning he arrived at work late, looking tired but happy.

"Sorry I'm late," he said, holding up his

wrists. They were covered with burn marks. "Got a bit tied up," he said, with a self-satisfied smile. "Bom."

Around that time I too became single, which compounded my money woes. My live-in boyfriend had moved out, leaving me with a small, sad record collection and a one-bedroom flat I couldn't afford on my own. It was Colin who came to my emotional rescue, and we bonded in mutual crisis, since his boyfriend had also left that night, following an argument. The difference was that while mine moved right in with the girl he'd been cheating with, Colin's returned the following morning, begging to be taken back. I soon learned this was a recurring drama played out by Colin and his boyfriend, a pouty male model who used too much hair gel.

"You need to earn more money," Colin advised me. "How about bar work? The pay's not bad with tips, and you might even meet some straight guys that way."

It was a good suggestion, but I still looked underage by several years and had enough trouble getting served in a pub let alone being allowed to work in one. But I knew I had to come up with something, and fast.

Since I spent all day on my feet in the shop,

I decided that an evening job where I could relax, reading or watching TV, would be ideal. So I decided to revisit the realm of babysitting, something I'd done a lot of in my early teens. I placed an ad on a card in a local shop window, and the following evening received my first call. The voice was male, and because my father had brought me up solo after my mother died, I immediately felt an affinity with him.

"I, er... Saw your ad," he stammered. "For a babysitter?"

"That's right," I said, hoping I sounded kind and encouraging. "I'm a babysitter."

"How old are you? You said nineteen in your ad?"

"Yes," I said. "But I like to think I'm quite mature. I work full-time during the day, but I'm trying to earn a bit of extra money in the evenings. I love children and do have quite a bit of experience." There was a pause. "How old are your kids?" I continued. "Or do you only have one?"

"Just one big one," he said, with strange emphasis on the word *big*.

"Okay," I said. "And how old is...he?"

"Can I just ask how much you charge?" said the man. I had previously resolved to set my fee at a decent rate, but I felt sorry for this guy, this poor single dad with the strapping son who was eating through his meagre weekly wages.

"Two pounds an hour," I said magnanimously. There was a click. "Hello?" I said. "Hello?"

It was a while before I realized what had happened. I felt my face redden as I wondered if he'd understood the true nature of the mix-up, or thought that my rate reflected my being the worst prostitute in town. The next caller came straight to the point.

"My nappy is full," he growled. A suitable response eluded me, but at least this time I had the wherewithal to hang up on him. I got two more enquiries that night, both men, but this time I was ready.

"Just to clarify, I am interested only in *real* babysitting work," I said before they could tell me what they were looking for. "You know, babies, toddlers – *actual* children. My rate is four pounds an hour." Click. Click.

The next day I went to the newsagents to retrieve my card from the window, even though I'd paid for it to be displayed for two weeks. Before entering the shop, I paused and read a few of the other cards around it, immediately regretting not having done this before placing my ad. "*Private schooling by Nancy. Strict but loving discipline*," read one. "*French Polish by Chantal,*" read another, "*I pay attention to every detail.*" Suddenly my innocent words transformed into pure euphemism: "*Mature 19-year-old seeks evening babysitting work. Reliable, trustworthy and experienced.*" I blushed, entered and asked the lady for my card back.

If we'd had the Internet and craigslist back then, things might have been different, both for me and, especially, for Patrick. As it was, we were the only two Peacock employees who lived alone, so Patrick best understood my financial predicament and offered me the most practical advice. He told me that if I phoned the city council, I could probably get my flat rent-adjusted and controlled, just as he'd done. I followed his advice and a man came over, poked around my flat and wrote some notes. A couple of weeks later I received a letter notifying me that my rent was being reduced by sixty pounds a month, which I still couldn't afford.

There were two cash registers in the shop, one near each door. The main one, close to the front entrance and adjacent to the changing rooms, was usually busy and always manned by at least two employees. The one near the rear doors was quieter and more isolated. We took reluctant turns over there, in "solitary confinement" as we called it, standing alone behind the counter, dusting jewellery, waiting for clients and wishing our lives away.

It was on such a shift that I went astray. I had taken a notebook with me and was composing a bad poem about being bored and wishing my life away when a frumpy young woman approached, brandishing a pink and red puffball skirt. We had just taken delivery of a rack of puffball skirts in various two-tone colour combinations, two seasons after they had gone out of fashion and six months after Princess Diana had been snapped by the paparazzi wearing one.

"How much are these?" she asked.

"Nineteen ninety-nine."

"I'll take it," she said, handing me a twenty-pound note. She obviously hadn't tried it on, or she wouldn't have been buying it. Even Princess Di looked bad in a puffball skirt. I took the cash, put it in the till, handed her a penny change and bagged up the voluminous garment. She left. Then I realized I'd forgotten one crucial step of the transaction: the receipt. And the reason there was no receipt was that I had not rung up the item in the till, which had for some reason been already open, drawer ajar.

My criminal mind, dormant for so long, began to stir. And my devilish inner voice was already at work, reminding me of my extreme poverty and reasoning that the deed was already done, and besides, who'd be hurt? Who'd even know? I looked around to make sure nobody was watching. Colin and Mel were over at the other till, busy with a queue of customers. Patrick was in his section, swatting a Persian carpet. I pressed "no sale" and the till drawer shot open. My clammy fingers closed on the twenty. I pulled it out and slipped it under my jumper, tucking it into the top of my tights. This instantly triggered abstract images of rattling Smarties and angry shopkeepers. To quash these unpleasant recollections, I thought positively about how this money would prevent me from plunging into debt, at least for a couple of days.

After that I looked forward to my shifts at the quiet cash desk, even offering to cover for others who were only too willing to give up three hours of extreme boredom. It was so easy. If a customer came back for a forgotten receipt (and they rarely did,) I simply pretended to have mislaid it and rang in the items "again." But I was careful not to become foolhardy, confining myself to a couple of items a day, and never doing it two days in a row.

One night I got a scare when Shadia re-emerged from cashing up the day's takings.

"It's so weird," she said. "I've counted three times and we're seven pence out. This isn't the first time either; it's happened before." I knew then that I had to be more careful, and more cunning. I didn't steal anything for a few days after that; then, when I was sure Shadia had forgotten about the discrepancies, and when greed and need again got the better of me, I started pilfering once more. Now, though, I made certain I had pennies on me to replace the ones I was giving to customers, thus ensuring the float would balance.

It was, therefore, a complete shock when Colin rushed over one morning and told me in an urgent whisper to take an unprecedented second tea break. I knew at once something serious was up.

"Why?" I said. "What's happened?"

"Nothing," he replied, about to erupt. "Oh all right, I just can't not tell you," he gushed. "We've got a tea leaf in our midst! The undercover cops are here to flush whoever it is out."

I felt faint and hoped Colin mistook the tremor in my voice for excitement.

"You're joking," I said. "Do you have any idea who it is?"

"Oh yes, we *know* who it is," said Colin. "We just need to prove it." *Oh dear God*, I thought.

"Really? Who?" I persisted. He shook his head; he'd said too much already. I wondered if he was toying with me, if he already knew that I was the tea leaf and was trying to wear me down, to force a confession out of me.

"Go and take your break," he said. "In fact, make it an early lunch. Hopefully they'll catch the thief while you're out, hand in till."

I left the store quickly, head down, unseeing, my mind spinning. Perhaps he was messing with me. But if they were really trying to catch the shoplifter red-handed and suspected me, then surely they wouldn't have sent me away like that? In which case, perhaps I still had a chance of getting away with it. After all, Colin had said that they knew who it was but still needed to prove it.

As I walked, I prayed silently and maniacally, offering things like Eternal Good Behaviour and doing Something Really Worthwhile with my life, like making an Important Global Contribution, in exchange for getting away with this one small — all right, medium-sized – offence.

It was early May, that period between spring and summer when English weather is at its most dodgy. The sun had just taken another break and a light drizzle was falling. Everything was grey. I took the road to the seafront, hoping the damp, salty air would help clear my head. The pungent odour of seaweed mingled with the smell of cod and chips, and my eyes stung as I pictured myself incarcerated, recalling this complex aroma as representational of Freedom Lost.

I walked quickly eastwards, past the main pier with its novelty photo booths and arcade games, past the ice cream stands and pebbly beaches, and continued until I reached the farthest flung and most famous pebbly beach of them all, which had opened seven years previously, designated for naturists. The initial hullabaloo had long since died down, but the fully clothed male onlookers perched on the wall above the nudist beach still tended to outnumber the naked people trying to have fun on it.

Today there were just two men on the wall, both wearing stereotypical dirty raincoats, but then again it was actually raining. They were staring, without enthusiasm, at the one diehard naturist who'd made an appearance, a shrivelled old man with wispy white hair. He was running about all over the place, probably in an attempt to keep warm. I looked at my watch, turned around and headed back for the store and my certain doom, my hair flattened, dark and dripping. I realized that I now looked how I felt: like a drowning rat.

Colin met me at the rear entrance, bouncing with the need to tell me the latest. "It's all over," he said. *Oh dear God, here we go,* I thought.

"What do you mean, 'over'?" I said carefully.

"The thief. Caught red-handed," said Colin. My brain had been attempting to shut down and now I scrambled to reactivate it in order to make sense of what he was saying.

"But I wasn't even —" I began, but luckily some slightly less stupid part of myself made me shut up. Colin was giddy with it all so didn't seem to notice.

"I mean, where is...?"

"Downstairs," said Colin. "Manager's office, being interviewed. And arrested, I imagine."

"Right. Wow." It was all I could manage.

Colin put me on the backdoor cash desk for the rest of the day. From my place of exile, repentant and alone, I reflected on my lucky escape and said silent prayers of thanks, reiterating that I'd meant what I said earlier about Never Doing Bad Again and instead Doing Something Really Good and Important. The few customers I had that afternoon might have found my style of cashiership a bit ostentatious: the receipt torn off with a flourish, then offered with a loud, "Would you like your receipt in the bag, Madam?" Some time passed before I realized that I didn't yet know whom they'd caught, I'd been so focused on the fortuitous fact that it wasn't me.

The culprit's identity was soon revealed: Patrick ascended the stairs slowly, surrounded by plainclothes and uniformed police officers. His head hung low and it looked like he was crying, or trying not to. In the background, fittingly, the song "Boys Don't Cry" by The Cure was playing. Well, it was either that or "Faith" by George Michael – the store's ancient sound system had eaten all but those two tapes.

As he passed by, Patrick lifted his head and looked me right in the eyes. I forced myself not to flinch or look away, feeling guiltier than ever and unbearably weak, for a better person would surely confess and shoulder the punishment alongside her fellow criminal. But I was spineless and self-preservation kept me mute.

As soon as I saw his face clearly it was obvious that Patrick hadn't shed any tears. In fact, he looked neither upset nor contrite but was smiling – just a little, almost a smirk. I lifted my hand in a feeble half-wave and smiled back. I was trying to convey kinship, encouragement and apology. He nodded his head, then jutted out his chin and jerked it a couple of times, while also raising and lowering his eyebrows, as if indicating something that he wanted me to notice and acknowledge.

It was only then that I fully took in his situation. Patrick was handcuffed to a young and very handsome uniformed policeman. His smile spread into a grin and he winked at me theatrically. Then, as the hunky cop led him out of the store Patrick said, very softly, "Bom."

TRIPE AND ONIONS

Meredith watched, spellbound, as the package of tripe shimmied towards her. It was the only item on the conveyor belt moving autonomously, a quivering cube of translucence, its slimy off-white contents encased in see-through plastic. It wobbled from side to side in time to the Muzak. Every second beat it caught the glare of the overhead strip lights and emitted a little glint.

In Meredith's field of vision, the vibrating package loomed large, dwarfing the tins of baked beans, tomato soup and cat food that had gathered in its shadow. She gripped her scanner gun more tightly and noted with rising panic that the bar code was not showing. She might actually have to touch the product.

Not for the first time, she regretted having slept through her alarm three weeks ago, thus missing her scheduled interview at the giant new MegaMart, which had sprung up, seemingly overnight, on the outskirts of town. At the time she'd not been that sorry – she wasn't crazy about MegaMart's orange Day-Glo uniforms, nor the idea of having to take three buses to work. But right now she wished she were dressed like a neon tangerine in a state-of-the-art supermarket with state-of-the-art flatbed scanners and state-of-the-art staff recreational facilities, including two pool tables and a subsidized restaurant offering free cappuccinos and muffins to all employees.

Instead she was here, in the shabby old Quik-Stop with its outdated cash registers and ancient scanner guns that were always malfunctioning, wearing a filthy blue and white smock and with only a fifteen-minute tea break in the cupboard they called a canteen to look forward to. Actually, she was looking forward to her tea break today because this afternoon it coincided with Jamie's.

She'd been fantasizing about how it would go all day. Jamie would be sitting on the only chair at the pull-down shelf table, frowning and pushing back his floppy hair as he concentrated on filling in the quick crossword in the *Mirror*.

Jamie was a couple of years older than she was and clever as well as cute – he had passed five GCSEs without even studying and gone on to do a whole year of A levels. He said he might go to university some day, although he also said he was already a student at the University of Life. He said that this was just a job but that he was thinking of applying for shift manager, at which point it might turn into a career, at least for a while. He said doing puzzles was like taking your brain to the gym.

She would enter the tiny room silently, allowing the *Intimately Beckham for Her* perfume sampler that she'd daubed herself with before leaving the house this morning to announce her presence. He would look up. She would already be at the sink with her back to him, and would take her time washing and rinsing one of three cracked cups that the Quik-Stop employees had to share, allowing him to take in her best feature, the long dark hair which hung in a lustrous ponytail down the centre of her back and ended on the swell of her bottom. His eyes would then travel down to the above-the-knee reveal of her shapely, smooth-shaven legs, which would not look too blotchy. He would be intrigued by the sterling silver-plated charm bracelet that looped around her left ankle, glittering across her only tattoo so far – a blue koi fish in a half-curl, slightly smudgy at the dorsal fin. All this was showcased by a kitten-heeled sandal – high enough to enhance her curvy physique, low enough that she could stand for eight hours straight without being in complete agony.

At last she would turn around, gracefully, and their eyes would meet. Their attraction would be so intense he wouldn't even notice her acne, her retainer or her puppy fat. What happened next changed every time she thought about it.

Sometimes he flushed and looked away (so cute!) only to be compelled, moments later, to glance back at her again and find her still looking down at him, seductive yet demure. Then, without relinquishing her gaze again, he would rise, advance with a small step and press his lips decisively against hers.

Sometimes he would admire her tattoo, tell her it was "kicking" and ask if it meant she was Pisces (it did). Then he would reveal he was Scorpio (but with Cancer rising so the idea of staying in some nights and/or settling down to a life of domestic bliss held heaps of appeal for him). Anyway, however it played out they couldn't help but acknowledge their water sign compatibility. Then he would read their daily horoscopes from the paper, and after he'd said the words "your soul mate is right under your nose and this weekend is the perfect time to at long last ignite your mutual passion," they would look at each other and laugh, in a sexy, knowing way, and then there'd be a pause during which they'd just stare at each other, letting the sexual tension in the room reach unbelievably unbearable proportions.

Sometimes she would say something dead funny and smart, which would make him laugh and realize that she had brains and wit as well as natural beauty. Then he would pull her onto his lap, both of them laughing, in a sexy, knowing way.

And sometimes he would simply declare his undying love for her, with great seriousness, and ask her to go to see a movie with him on Saturday night, or just stay in and watch telly together, and be his proper, official girlfriend.

The customer had finished unloading all her groceries and was looking at Meredith expectantly. The package of tripe had, for the moment, stopped moving.

"'Lo," muttered Meredith, making fleeting mandatory eye contact with the old woman, who had mauve-rinsed hair, a powdery apricot complexion and thin lips rendered no fuller by their coat of fuchsia goop. Tabby hairs sprouted all over her sweater and a few more clung to her lime green neckerchief. The child seat of her cart was occupied by a balled up, see-through, crinkly raincoat and plastic headscarf, both beaded with raindrops.

Meredith had served this old lady before, many times, but didn't know her name. Quik-Stop staff members were encouraged to address regulars by name. Sharon would know, as would Annie, and even Jamie, although if he didn't he'd simply call her "Darling" or "Gorgeous" and wink at her, and she'd leave the store charmed and giggling. At least, that's what Jamie would have done before he got caught not charging one of the elderly regulars for pet food and got taken off the checkouts and relegated permanently to stacking shelves. He was lucky not to have been fired; the branch manager, known by the staff as Bony Tony, was in the process of doing just that when Dippy Deb, the area manager, had inexplicably intervened. Anyway, Meredith wished the clientele had to wear name tags too.

"Good afternoon, Meredi!" Meredith was reminded that this customer always misread, or at least mispronounced, her name. She wondered if it was a question of shortsightedness or an inability to pronounce the "th."

"This is the third day of non-stop rain," said the old lady cheerfully. "And it's supposed to go on like this until Thursday. Then we're in for some thunderstorms."

"Yeah?" said Meredith miserably, wondering if pointing out the nearby carousel of cheap reading glasses would seem rude. The old bat's poor eyesight could have its uses, though – perhaps she would knock something over, a chocolate bar from the stands or one of her own purchases. Meredith contemplated surreptitiously pushing one of the tins over the edge herself. If something would only fall off and get a bit bashed up, she would be able to press the intercom button, which activated the store's ancient PA system, lean into the microphone and announce, in her deepest, sexiest voice, "Code Four Grocery. There's been a droppage at checkout number two. Product damaged, replacement required. Thank you." Then Jamie would stop stocking the shelves in aisle number seven and would race over, pick up the dented can, run off to get a replacement, run back and hand it to Meredith with a sexy smile. As she took the can from him, their fingers would touch and he would notice how beautifully manicured her hand was, how glossy her nails.

"Oh yes!" The old woman was delighted to have been fed the right cue. "But we mustn't grumble, must we? Because it's *good* news for the plants!" As she chattered on about the window boxes at her new flat, which were much less work than her old garden had been (although she did miss it sometimes), but which kept her very busy (because they held such an array of flowers and herbs), Meredith scanned her purchases. As she dispensed with the canned goods and moved through the perishable items (a pint of full-cream milk, three small potatoes, two medium-sized onions, one large carrot and a fistful of wilting parsley) she gradually decreased her speed.

At last only the package of tripe remained, trembling slightly. The conveyor belt and Meredith were motionless. The old lady leaned forward. Her manner was conspiratorial; her faded grey eyes twinkled with girlish glee. "I'm treating myself," she stage-whispered. "Having a bit of tripe and onions for my tea."

Meredith responded with a nod but couldn't manage even the spectre of a smile. Long-repressed childhood memories flooded her mind and her senses felt assaulted anew as she recalled the sight, smell, taste and texture of her late grandmother's relentless recipes: tongue sandwiches, neck stew, fried liver, steak and kidney pie.

Granny McDuff had been a strict but loving old omnivore from the "waste not, want not" generation who could – and did – cook any part of an animal and eat it with gusto, and expected her overindulged grandchildren to do the same. Even the aroma of a newly opened tin of cat food made her salivate and purr excitedly.

"Beautiful," she would say, putting down the can opener and taking a long, deep sniff. "Those Whiskas people must be trained chefs. I'd happily eat this for *my* supper."

Mr. Tibbins would look up and fix his wild green eyes on Granny McDuff. He would press his moist nose into one of her sizeable calves and spread the wetness with his muzzle, tracing the line of a spider vein. Then he would snake round and around her lumpy legs, mewing anxiously, dusting her swollen ankles with his flickering tail, his cries growing more and more desperate.

At the dinner table, Granny McDuff was always perplexed by her family's lack of enthusiasm.

"You youngsters are so fussy," she would say. "I'd swap you a bit of lean for that nice juicy piece of fat in a heartbeat. Now tuck in, it's getting cold."

"Cold-*er*," Meredith's younger sister Alison would whisper, sticking her fingers in her mouth, and she and Meredith would use their big cloth napkins to hide their giggles, as well as the lumps of grey gristle. Their grandmother continued to chew her meat slowly, lips pursed, making little wet clicks of disapproval (or ecstasy, depending on who or what had her attention).

Sometimes she would uncover the hidden morsels of boiled flesh, tearing open the girls' crumpled napkins to reveal meaty gobs of glue. She would unstick them one by one, pulling them away from the fabric. Then she would place them back on the girls' plates, fold her arms and raise her eyebrows expectantly. Meredith and Alison would fold their arms too and stare glumly at the globules, which were by now stone cold and faintly furry with linen fluff. It was a standoff, which usually ended after about twenty minutes, when Granny McDuff either fell asleep or had to go and empty her small, irritable bladder.

Their struggles had finally ceased when Meredith announced, at age twelve, that she was turning vegan. She had just read and been inspired by a double-page feature in a magazine about the surprising number of celebrities who'd become veggie. She'd been drawn to the article by the cover tease: "How does Brad resemble a rabbit? Hint: It's not what you're thinking!!!" The list included Brad, Orlando Bloom, Pamela Anderson and Meatloaf. She didn't know for sure who Meatloaf was, but she totally got the irony.

Her mother had been uncharacteristically supportive of her decision but was also concerned about protein intake, so Meredith compromised and became an ovo-lacto-vegetarian.

"Vegetables aren't enough for a growing

lass," Granny McDuff had said gravely after being apprised of the new situation. "You'll waste away. Alone. Mark my words: Lads don't want skin and bones, they want a bit of meat on their lasses."

"I'm still eating eggs," Meredith had responded. "And cheese."

"Cheese doesn't count."

"And avocados. And cake."

"You're already as pale as a parsnip. Let's just hope that this is one of those passing phases. Your mother was afflicted with those too, I wish I could say briefly."

Yet to Meredith's surprise, Granny McDuff had catered actively to her passing phase, regularly whipping up cheese omelettes and mushroom quiches, and making her traditional Sunday spotted dick with sunflower oil. On Meredith's sixteenth birthday, last year, Granny McDuff had produced a special version of toad-in-the-hole with Twiglets standing in as rather skinny "toads." And every year, she made two Christmas puddings, one using fake suet.

For the first time, Meredith became conscious that next Christmas would be the first without Granny McDuff and therefore the first without a fruity, brandy-drenched vegetarian pudding unless she somehow got it together to make one herself. She was pretty sure she'd be on a diet by then anyway.

Meredith reached out gingerly and grasped a corner of the plastic package between her thumb and forefinger. It occurred to her that even Granny McDuff had never attempted to serve a dish made from stomach lining. Slowly, she lifted the bag slightly and, as she did so, the sticky contents heaved and shifted. She felt her own stomach lurch but managed to quash both her gag reflex and her impulse to let go of the package. Instead, she tightened her grip, her eyes darting across the undulating underbelly, searching for the bar code. At last she spotted it, dead centre. Turning it over was indeed unavoidable.

Suppressing a shudder, Meredith closed her eyes as she flipped over the package. She opened them again just in time to see the tripe complete its somersault and land half on, half off the inner edge of the conveyor belt. There, it hesitated for a moment before slipping over the side, plunging inexorably towards her feet. Like a front seat passenger in a car accident, Meredith experienced the next three seconds in extreme slow motion.

On impact, the packaging burst and the slow motion spell was broken. Meredith's strappy sandals offered little protection from the dreaded contents. Her toes, their nails perfectly painted in sparkly vermilion, curled in a futile attempt to duck and cover. There was no escape down there. The opaque sludge spewed up and out in a thick, cloudy fountain, coating everything under the counter.

Meredith looked down at the horror below, and her nostrils registered the stench of raw offal. She jerked her head upwards, gulping for air and reached for the conveyor belt to steady herself. The customer's aged, liver-spotted hand was already there. It gave her a reassuring squeeze.

Instead of recoiling, Meredith squeezed back and smiled at the old lady — really smiled — for the first time. If it wasn't for the conveyor belt separating them, she might have given in to her urge to fall into the old lady's spindly arms and get lost in a replenishing cuddle. Instead she made do with the clasp, which conveyed empathy as well as plain comfort. They were in it together and the worst had already happened.

Soon it would be over. Everything was going to be all right.

A tugging, pinching sensation alerted her to the fact that the old lady was trying to extricate herself. Meredith let go, blinking back tears. They were both still smiling.

"Oh dear," said the old woman, and beneath the still-honeyed tones Meredith could detect something flinty and unyielding. "I do hope that wasn't the last bag of tripe."

"Oh," said Meredith. "No. I don't know. I'll have to check."

Slowly, she reached for the intercom button. Her feet were slimy and cold; it reminded her of standing in the shallows of a lake. She hated lakes with their shifting, sludgy bottoms at the edge and creepy, endless depths in the middle, their leeches, electric eels and monstrous others, but she would have preferred to be in one than here. She checked her watch. Twenty minutes until her tea break.

She glanced over at the automatic exit. The double doors were stuck, half-open, for the third time that week. In the potholed parking lot beyond, heavy rain continued to fall. She could make a run for it and be outside in seconds. She'd be free out there—free to scream and free to cry. She imagined splashing in a rain puddle until her feet were washed clean. She imagined her tears mingling with the raindrops so nobody could tell she was even crying. There was a whooshing sensation inside her head.

Slowly, she depressed the red button, leaning into the microphone.

"Code Four Grocery," she said, her crackling echo reverberating around the supermarket. "There's been a droppage at checkout number two. Code Four Grocery, please. Product damaged, replacement required. And there's also been a...slight spillage, so...cleanup is also needed. Thank you."

She straightened up. Her fingers were glistening. She wiped her hands on her smock and tucked a stray hair behind her ear. Then she stood and waited, listening to the rhythmic drumming of the rain on the corrugated roof and the patter of Jamie's footsteps.

ACKNOWLEDGEMENTS

I am indebted to everyone who read and gave feedback on early versions of these stories during workshops at: the QWF with JPF, our spin-off writers' group and Concordia University, in particular: Mira Cuturilo, Carrie Haber, Kasia Juno and Julie McIsaac. Very special thanks to Mikhail Iossel. Special thanks to Sue Lee Sekulic. Cheers to Holly Alexander and her mum for the phrase "tall food." Sincere thanks to Mike O'Connor, Dan Varrette and everyone at Insomniac. Grateful thanks to Gillian Rodgerson for sterling copy editing. Very special thanks to my amazing editor and cover designer, Jon Paul Fiorentino.

I would also like to acknowledge all my wonderful friends and family on both sides of the Atlantic. I am especially grateful to my husband, Alan Best, for his unerring love, support and encouragement and to our two incredible, inspiring children, Eleanor and Nathaniel.